THE *e*-ENTITY

The *e*-Entity

Printed in Canada

ISBN 0-595-47525-6

Graphic layout by Jason Kane

Copyright © 2007 Casey A. Johnson
www.caseyajohnson.com

All rights reserved. No part of this book may be used or reproduced in any manner whatsoever without written permission except in the case of brief quotations embodied in critical articles or reviews.

For Dillon:
Your creation was my salvation

Whoso loves, believes the impossible –
Elizabeth Barrett Browning

ACKNOWLEDGMENTS:

Anne Johnson, my mentor, mother, friend, inspiration and life-line. Thank you for encouraging me to always follow my dreams.

Eva Fisher, my Swedish connection. Thank you for my Swedish 101 lessons and for not laughing………too hard.

Andrew Jankowski, you have inspired me from the first day we met. I am honoured to have been taught by you.

Jessie Johnson, my grandmother. Thank you for your unwavering faith in me.

Gary Smith, my dad, you will always be my hero.

Elizabeth Northrup, thank you for your continual support and encouragement. I am proud you are part of my family.

Mikey & Kiki, you are the best siblings anyone could ever have.

Erroll Fisher, because I appreciate you and because I would never hear the end of it.

Peter Urwin, they say even in the briefest encounters you can still make a profound impact on someone's life. Thanks for the push.

Joy Shikaze, MJS Communications. You have been brilliant to work with.

Reid Turnbull, thank you for your support and for keeping it honest.

PROLOGUE

It all started with a simple online introduction. That was it. No grand gesture, no majestic prose, no extended effort. It had never occurred to me those few simple words would be the catalyst to the most monumental and shocking event of my life.

I am still recovering from it – both mentally and physically. The lies, the danger, the deceit, it is still so inconceivable to me. Even the highest levels of government knew nothing about it. That's how deep the cover-up went.

His name was Thomas, and he was the most incredible man I had ever encountered. Even from ten thousand kilometres away, he was still able to capture me immediately and completely.

I had been single for four years. I was past the age of wanting to be picked up at a bar and under the age of wanting to sit at home every weekend watching television and complaining about the weather. So following in the footsteps of twenty-million people, I decided to try online dating.

After all, it is the age of cyber dating.

What better way to meet someone – pre-screened, pre-selected, and custom made right down to location, age, height, weight, zodiac sign, hobbies, you name it. My logic dictated I would probably save myself endless hours of erroneous first dates that would most likely never progress past the first one. It would also save me from that insufferable drunk at the end of the bar who always found me completely irresistible. I wasn't looking for a serious commitment, just someone to spend a bit of time with and break up the monotony.

Accordingly, I set out on a mission to customize a search for my ideal man, or as close as I could get. I read through what seemed like hundreds of online bios, all attached to hopeful faces and all apparently searching for either a date, marriage or an intimate encounter.

By a sheer twist of fate, I found him. The perfect man. Three days later, I was smack dab in the middle of the most quixotic adventure of my life. But something was wrong. I wish I had known then what I know now. Women have the best intuition in the world. Those instincts should never be ignored.

CHAPTER 1

I sat staring into nothingness hoping I could motivate myself to write this analysis on the latest skirmish in North Korea, but I could not even manage a spark of interest. It was not the subject matter that disinterested me. In fact, nothing about being a journalist and being able to shed some light on the atrocities of war could ever disinterest me. It was simply the sheer idea of sitting still for more than five minutes that stifled my brain, especially when I had to write follow-up analyses to my stories. I missed being in the field. I missed the excitement, the challenge, the adrenaline rush of fighting for the underdogs and going to battle for them through the media. My assignments were simple. Fly into post-war countries, still swathed in the aftermath of combat, and give a voice to the people, the casualties, and the victims. Write about their lives, their experiences, and their anguish. Let those at home see the real story.

I had been back in Canada for about a month after being gone for almost a year. I knew it was time to come home. I was in genuine need of feeding my homesickness. During my last month in Pyongyang, I started dreaming about all the wonderfully mundane things life had to offer. I dreamt about ordering a pound of air-chilled Atlantic salmon from the local grocery store. I imagined chatting with my next-door neighbour, Mrs. Goldman, and discussing the skill of creating the perfect-coloured tulip. I fantasized about waking up in a warm and cosy bed that smelled of lilac fabric softener. But now I was back, I was starting to go stir crazy. I guess my brain had a one-month expiration date when it came to the effects of daily monotony.

The nothingness was starting to addle my brain, so I decided to stretch my legs and wander downstairs away from the confines of my home office and into the kitchen to pour myself a large glass of my favourite Wolf Blass Cabernet Sauvignon. As I reached for the bottle, I looked at the digital clock that was perched on the back of my stove. It read 10:43 a.m. It was still morning? I could have sworn it was at least mid-afternoon by now. So, I settled for a cool glass of cranberry juice instead. Perhaps Mr. Blass and I would enjoy each other's company later. It was my weakness, red wine. Well, good red wine. I thoroughly enjoyed it, especially with a good meal. The right glass of wine could even enhance the flavours of the most unsavoury meals. That was a little trick my ex taught me. I never did figure out whether he shared that tidbit of information with me in broad conversation or because of my culinary skills.

I sat down near the full-length glass doors in my living room, the ones that overlooked the escarpment. The scenery I found in Dundas was only one of the reasons I decided to live here. I also loved the people. The community still had that small town atmosphere, despite its recent growth in population.

My house was built with an open-concept, a must for me. I hated feeling boxed in and this was the perfect two-thousand-square-foot sanctuary. It was small enough that cleaning it wasn't too much of a chore; yet, it was still big enough for me to totter around in without feeling claustrophobic. Besides, I really didn't need anything bigger. I always seemed to be out of Canada longer than I was in it.

From the corner of my eye, I caught the leaves of the southern catalpa trees gently blowing in the breeze. I turned my head to watch them. That was my favourite colour of green – that fusion of olive shades that melded together so brilliantly, changing hues with each tiny burst of air stream. I sighed, deeply filling my lungs with air-conditioned coolness and rested my head on the wall beside me. Atop the escarpment, I watched as two red-tailed hawks soared just above the treetops. They must be mates, I thought. Hawks usually flew solo. A sense of peace flowed through me as I sipped at my cranberry juice and watched them. Somehow, they just made me feel composed, calm, centred. A drop of condensation dripped from my glass onto my bare leg just as I heard the doorbell chime. I stood up to get it, wiping off my leg in the process, and put my cranberry juice down on the floor beside my chair. I laughed for probably the hundredth time. Who on earth would invent a doorbell that chimed to the tune of *When the Saints go Marching In*? Nothing says welcome like a New Orleans' funeral march. I wanted to install one that chimed to the tune of *The Stripper* just for the sheer entertainment value. I could only imagine the look on the mail carrier's face.

I opened up the front door and the wall of moisture that hit me was immense. It actually felt like someone had thrown wet paper towels all over my body. It was nearly thirty five degrees Celsius already and the humidity was going to be sheer torture again today. It was the kind of heat that crushed your lungs with every breath. I could not remember Southern Ontario ever being this hot and humid. Then again, maybe it was just the care-free memories of childhood I was, or was not, remembering.

"Whew. I think I lost ten pounds from the car to here," Marianne said.

"Isn't it awful?" I replied. "So? How are things with you?"

"Not bad, not bad," Marianne said, as she walked into my foyer, took off her shoes and sighed as her bare feet met the cool comfort of my Italian ceramic floors. "I just signed a new client."

"Excellent."

Marianne worked in the publishing industry. She was one of the most sought after literary agents in the country. We walked up the stairs and into the cool confines of my living room and sat down, while the gentle hum of the air conditioner breached the silence of the room.

"Can I get you an iced tea or cranberry juice?" I asked.

"Just water, if you don't mind."

I left Marianne sitting on my chaise longue and went to get her some water.

"So, how's the analysis coming along?" she yelled towards the kitchen.

"I don't know," I yelled back. "I can't seem to settle my brain long enough to delve into it."

I walked back into the living room and handed her a bottle of spring water.

"I thought you'd be savouring domestic bliss for a while yet. Don't tell me you're bored already?"

I sat down on the over-stuffed chair across from her, picked up my cranberry juice and crossed my legs in an attempt to get comfortable again.

"You know me too well," I said, laughing.

"Hey, I know you better than you know yourself," Marianne said, with a wink.

She was right. We had been friends for a long time and no one knew me better than she did. We always joked with one another saying we had so much ammunition on each other we had to stay friends. I also trusted her explicitly – a mark of distinction I could offer no other. My past was riddled with distrust. I thought perhaps that was why I sought refuge in the midst of beleaguered countries, ones that allowed me to get so caught up in their angst I had little time to think of my own. I wasn't unhappy, exactly. In fact, I was quite happy with most aspects of my life. I just didn't like my past. It always seemed to hover above me like an ominous weight.

"Earth to Frankie," Marianne said, waving her hand in the air.

"Sorry. Where were we?"

"Listen, perhaps you need to find yourself a distraction. Something to help you relax. Something to perhaps *ground* you a bit?" Marianne said, again with a wink. Marianne was a big winker.

"Something?" I said derisively. "Oh, like I can't see right through that comment. You don't have to go around the houses, Mare. I pretty much get the picture. It's not the first time I've heard this from you."

"Okay, so I think you should meet someone. Would that be so bad?"

"Actually, it wouldn't. In fact, I've already put those wheels in motion, but not on the same scale you were thinking. I was just hoping for a bit of a distraction, that's all. Nothing too serious, just some good conversation and a bit of company. I don't think sitting at home for the last month has done me any favours. I miss the air of testosterone," I said, sweeping my hand up in front of my face and inhaling deeply. "You know, strong in limb and wind, deep voices, tantalizingly musky scents?"

"Hey, you could always wear one of these," Marianne said, as she held up a sterling silver charm that hung from her necklace.

"What is it?" I asked, bending forward to get a better look at the symbol.

"It's called a Seeker Charm. This one means, *Seeking Men.*"

"It's quite lovely. Perhaps I will invest in one, but in the meantime, I have something else lined up."

"Okay, so what is it?" she asked, still smiling.

"I've signed up for online dating," I said, flashing her my pearly whites.

Marianne just sat there staring at me with her best poker face until she finally said, "I'm pleading the fifth."

"Okay, first of all the Fifth Amendment refers to criminal rights not to opinions about online dating," I said, laughing. "And second, we are in Canada. Perhaps you should quote something from the Charter of Rights and Freedoms."

"Charming," she said mockingly. "Like that smug attitude will land you a man."

I laughed.

"You know my schedule, Mare. This way would be very convenient and practical for me. At any rate, statistics show over twenty-million people are doing it."

"Yeah, but nineteen million of those people are using it as a way to hide behind a computer screen on purpose. Think about that, my friend."

"You are such a cynic!"

"Actually, I consider myself a pragmatist," she said, as she smiled and lifted her bottle of water towards me to say cheers.

"Same thing," I said. Then I winked.

CHAPTER 2

After Marianne left, I made my way back up to my office and logged on to the dating site I had registered with. I wasn't going to check it for a few days, fearing an empty inbox, but my curiosity got the better of me. Besides, I was bored again.

My ego was doing well, twelve responses in two days. Not bad for a first-timer, I thought; but, it took me exactly twenty minutes to dismiss them all.

I sat back to think for a moment. What was I really looking for? I knew what I wanted; I just didn't know what it was yet. I knew what kind of man I was attracted to; I just couldn't describe him. I laughed. Somehow, in my head, that made perfect sense.

I contemplated a more direct approach. Instead of waiting for someone to contact me, perhaps I should be performing the searches myself, I thought. There were a lot of details I could have included in my searches, but I settled on performing some general ones based solely on location, nothing more than one hundred kilometres away. I figured it might be kind of tricky dating a man in, let's say, Australia. But after a plethora of searches, and what seemed like a sea of bios later, I got quite discouraged. I didn't even come across one person who sounded remotely interesting to me. They all sounded so insipid, so superficial. If I had to read one more tedious bio or look at one more photo of some self-inflated man standing in front of his sports car donning a grin that screamed midlife crisis, I was going to up chuck. Then I came across a photo of a man sprawled across his bed with a headline that read, 'True Gentleman', and that did it. I pushed myself away from my desk and began to make my way back down stairs, shaking my head. I could not believe he actually thought women were attracted to that sort of thing.

As I entered my living room, I began to question my avenue of pursuit. Perhaps this was not the best way to find a date after all. Maybe I should just abandon my armoire full of little frilly lingerie and join a convent. Come to think about it, I might actually qualify for that by now. I also mulled over what Marianne had said. Her remarks were harder to ignore now I had feasted my eyes upon, 'True Gentleman.' Maybe I should just take up a hobby. Skeet shooting perhaps? Nothing lets you vent sexual frustration like blowing the crap out of little clay pigeons. But the fact of the matter was I never seemed to do anything by halves. I knew I would try again, and probably again, until I felt like I had exhausted all of my resources. I was almost certainly one of the most tenacious people on the planet. At least that's what I liked to call it. Men usually referred to it as being stubborn.

CHAPTER 3

Sunday was rainy, and I was a bit blue. The weather always had a profound affect on me. Perhaps rainy days were a subcategory of seasonal affective disorder, or at least that is what I think they called it. There seemed to be a name given to almost everything these days. I wondered what they'd call it if some overly analytical psychologist saw me talking to myself and laughing my butt off over what I had just said. You can bet it would end in 'affective disorder.'

With an optimistic hope of renewing my spirits, I made myself a cup of Earl Grey, steeped of course, and sat down in the living room. I turned on the television hoping to catch a football game. Well, I called it football. Most Canadians, and most Americans for that matter, referred to it as soccer. I remembered reading somewhere a man by the name of Charles Wreford-Brown coined the phrase as an abbreviation for Association Football in the 1800's. I never really understood why it stuck, or how he came up with that particular abbreviation. Even 'Assfoot' would have made a lot more sense to me. Oh well, the way I looked at it, men had the Playboy channel and I had football. I didn't care what they called it.

I picked up the converter and began to search through the stations. I could channel surf like a pro. It used to drive my grandmother batty. I could flip through the channels so fast, she said I could even put the healthiest person into an epileptic seizure.

Two hundred channels and twelve seconds later, I concluded there was nothing on to watch.

Okay, slight exaggeration.

I made my way back up the stairs to my office to check my e-mail, then maybe I would venture out to see a movie and have an early dinner with Marianne, if she wasn't busy. Even if she was, I wouldn't mind. I was one of those rare people who actually enjoyed their own company. I usually found myself a constant source of amusement.

I answered seven e-mails and Google'd some information for my analysis, but I lost interest again very quickly. This instant boredom was starting to get on my nerves.

Then I considered the dating site and thought perhaps I could pass a bit of time there. I decided to delve into some of the search categories instead. It was actually quite interesting. I went over all the criteria available and was absolutely amazed. It was kind of like creating your own human being, I thought, laughing.

"This must be just how Dr. Ian Wilmut and his Scottish colleagues felt when they cloned Dolly," I said aloud, utterly amused with myself.

I plunged in, expanded my geographical search area and chose over thirty distinctive traits, pretty much the maximum I could choose from. I also looked for an option regarding the quantity of body hair one might have, but there was no selection for that sort of thing. Quite pleased with myself, I hit the enter button. "Okay, let's just see what this bad-boy computer can produce for me."

At first I thought the computer might actually laugh back at me, but there it was – one hit.

I burst out laughing. This was too funny. I never expected to get a hit. This was turning out to be more fun than I thought. I clicked on his photo, but not before closing one eye and bracing myself for the obnoxious, smug grin that would probably ogle me from cyberspace. Then I paused. My god, he was beautiful. His opening caption read, "Whoso loves, believes the impossible."

Browning? He quoted Browning? Okay, this was absurd. My search was a joke. I was only aiming to amuse myself, not actually find a match. Truth be told, I was sort of looking for an excuse to pack it in, to throw in the proverbial towel and find an alternative means of searching. Tenacious or not, I was never truly comfortable with this avenue of meeting someone. Deep down I knew this probably wasn't the right venue for me. I think it was 'True Gentleman' that shone the light on that epiphany. That was one image I will never be able to erase from my mind, no matter how hard I try.

Still a bit perplexed, but admittedly curious, I dug in deeper and read his bio. It was brief and to the point, but at the same time it was also intelligible and interesting. I could tell by the way he wrote that he was well educated; but, he also seemed composed and confident somehow, if you can actually deduce those kinds of personality traits from a few words on a JavaScript page.

It all seemed a bit ludicrous, a bit nonsensical, but at the same time, I was dead curious. I mean, what did I have to lose? What was the worst thing that could happen? I couldn't help myself. I typed him a brief note introducing myself, gave him my IM address, and attached three photos of myself – ones that were particularly flattering, of course. Then I lifted my teacup and said, "No offence, Marianne, but here's to not being pragmatic." Then I hit send.

CHAPTER 4

Three days had passed and no response. I had almost given up on the whole thing but later that evening, as I was checking my e-mail, an instant message popped up on my screen.

"Hello, Bella."

I paused for a brief moment, let my brain register who it was, then I smiled and thought, "Nice opening line."

"Thank you for taking the time to contact me," he typed. "I am truly honoured."

"You're welcome."

I was determined to come across cool and aloof. You know, the way women think they can be while everyone else in the room can see right through them? Well, the other women in the room can anyway; men still think we're being genuine. No wonder they had a hard time figuring us out.

"Please, tell me what time it is where you are," he asked. I could almost hear his European accent coming through his words.

"It's 10:00 p.m. What time is it there and where are you?"

"It is 5:00 a.m. here. I am in a small village just outside of Beirut."

"Beirut? Your bio said you lived in England."

"This is true, but I am on assignment here for six more weeks."

"Assignment?"

"Yes. I sometimes volunteer."

"Volunteer at what, if you don't mind me asking."

"I am in the medical profession. I will explain the rest when we chat again. I am very sorry, but I have to run. When I saw you were online, I thought I should at least say a quick hello and say thank you for the e-mail. I will look for you again very soon, perhaps in the next day or two. Again, I apologize for such a brief encounter. The next time we chat, it will be longer, I promise."

"I'll look forward to it," I typed. "By the way, what's your name?"

"I am sorry. It is Thomas," he replied. "Your e-mail said your name was Frankie, yes? Is that a sobriquet for Francesca?"

"Yes, it is," I replied. "I was named after my great-aunt."

"That is a beautiful name. Italian?"

"She was, yes. I'm more of a Heinz 57, if you know what I mean."

"Heinz 57?" he typed.

I laughed.

"Italian, Polish, Spanish, Scottish, the list goes on," I explained.

"With 6.5 billion people on the planet, and such vast emigration, I think that is the norm today."

"Yes. I guess it is."

"I am very sorry, but I do have to run."

"No problem," I typed. "Until then, Thomas."

"Enjoy your evening. Sleep well."

And then he was gone.

Again, three days had passed until I heard from him again. He apologized for the lack of communication but said their Internet stability was uncertain at best, and that was on a good day. I didn't mind. It gave me the chance to work on this bloody analysis. I did, however, finally find out he was a surgeon and he volunteered his time as often as he could. Apparently, he had done quite a bit of travelling over the years and had volunteered all over the world.

It appeared gallantry was not dead.

Over the course of the next couple of weeks, our communications became more frequent. We chatted via the

Internet for endless hours, sometimes into the wee hours of the morning; and, I fell head-over-heels in love with his mind. He was the most intelligent and communicative man I had ever met. I wondered if it was indeed possible to fall in love with someone's mind. Grinning, I concluded it was and that I was perfectly sane and moved on.

Now, our conversations not only came by instant messaging, but also by elongated e-mails and, most recently, by phone. We were right in the middle of a very meticulous online conversation about how stunning I was, when in mid-sentence, he stopped what he was typing and wrote, "Surprise."

I sat puzzled for a moment, then five seconds later my phone rang. I froze. No, it couldn't be. I gave him my phone number a while ago, but I thought he'd only get the chance to use it once he got back to England, not from Lebanon. I don't know why it caught me off guard the way it did. I honestly felt a bit nervous and my stomach dropped. It was a bizarre feeling for me. I was an extrovert, outspoken, I loved to meet new people; and, I was rarely ever nervous around men – well, most men. I'd have a hard time keeping it together if Sean Connery landed on my doorstep, but that was different. He wasn't a man, he was a god.

The phone rang again. This time I decided it would be much better to answer it instead of just sitting there staring at it. I picked it up and said hello.

"Hello, Frankie."

"Thomas?" I said.

"I wanted to surprise you. I am so tired of chatting with you online and only being able to imagine what your voice sounds like," he said.

I couldn't respond immediately. I had the most ineffable feeling come over me. It was his voice. As soon as I heard it, my stomach dropped, but for a very different reason this time. I couldn't explain it. It was as if I was talking to a complete stranger. His voice definitely had a strong European accent, but it still sounded nothing like I had imagined. I knew it sounded crazy, and I wished I could explain it; but, it was such a powerful feeling I just couldn't ignore it. It was one of those situations where your head began to argue with your instincts and you had no control over them. It was a tumultuous battle between rationale and instinct.

"I'm glad you had the opportunity," I said, stumbling and not being able to fully concentrate on the conversation.

"This has made my day," he said, sounding quite pleased.

"You are too kind, Thomas. Thank you," I replied.

"I have to make this call quick. I was only granted a few minutes. Land lines are very precious here. I just wanted to hear your voice."

"I'm glad you called, Thomas. We'll chat again soon."

"Ciao, Bella."

After I hung up the phone, I sat staring at it. There was no way that voice belonged to Thomas. Admittedly, I had only seen one photo of him, the one he used on the dating site, but I still couldn't make the connection. The two just didn't seem to fit. I sat there shaking my head trying to make sense of it.

My laptop beeped and jarred me back to attention as an IM message popped up on my screen. It was Thomas. I forgot we were still online.

"It was very nice hearing your voice."

I stared at the screen before answering him. Was this what they called the fundamental female instinct, I wondered? I knew I had some pretty good instincts, my job demanded it and I learned to listen to them, but most of those were ones I could explain, at least with some sort of lucidity. But, this? It

The e-Entity

was a feeling based solely on a reaction to something totally intangible. A voice.

"Are you there?" My screen beeped again.

"Sorry," I typed, trying to think of an excuse for not answering him straight away. "It took me a minute to get back to the computer."

"Not to worry," he replied.

"Listen, Thomas, I was thinking. Do you have any photos you could send me? I'd really like to have some."

"Of course. I will find some and attach them to my next e-mail."

"That would be wonderful," I typed.

"I should go now. Have a wonderful evening and we will chat again tomorrow, yes?"

"Same time, same place," I typed.

"Take care."

"Yes, you too."

I logged off the computer and sat staring at it for a moment. This was crazy, I thought. Then, I began to mentally berate myself. How can you tell what someone's voice sounds like by a photo? It was preposterous. I knew a gut instinct should never be ignored, but there were also false alarms, weren't there? I was probably just paranoid. This was my first kick at the can at online dating. I was bound to feel a bit apprehensive. I also didn't think the chat I had with Marianne the other day helped. What was I thinking, exactly? That Thomas wasn't Thomas because his voice didn't match his picture? That was ridiculous. I was being ridiculous.

Before bed, I went online to check my e-mail. There were still some unanswered ones from work that needed my attention. I had been neglecting my work a bit and decided it was time to play catch up. When I clicked on my inbox, I noticed an e-mail from Thomas entitled, *Photos*.

That was quick, I thought.

His e-mail was the first one I opened. I clicked on the attachments and waited for them to download. As soon as they began to pop up on my screen, I began to scrutinize them very carefully. Three of them definitely resembled his photo on the dating site, there was no denying that, but strangely enough these ones looked like they were professionally taken. Of a model? Come to think of it, the one on the dating site was rather polished as well, but that one was only a head shot. These were full body length. The last two didn't quite seem to resemble the rest, but they were taken at rather odd angles, and a bit blurry, so it was very hard to tell who they resembled. I was totally confused now. I was also getting very frustrated with myself. Okay, so he took a really nice photo. So what? He could have had some professionally taken. I have. Why was I making such a big deal out of his voice for anyway? This was all getting a bit over the top, I thought. Thomas was definitely one of the most articulate men I had ever met. Our conversations could attest to that fact. Besides, it all came down to motivation really – everything always did. So what was Thomas's motivation? What could he possibly gain by sending me photos that were not of him? We were going to eventually meet one day and he knew it. I was just being absurd. It was time to put it out of my head.

CHAPTER 5

The next morning I woke to the sound of a lawnmower humming in the distance. Thank god I paid someone to do that for me, I thought, rolling over and tossing the feather pillow over my head. As I lay there, the hum of the two-stroke engine became louder. I knew I wasn't going to get much more sleep, so I decided to go for my run instead. I got up, got dressed and decided to check the weather before I ventured outside. As soon as I opened the front door, I knew.

"Okay, so today we use the indoor treadmill," I said aloud.

After my four kilometre run, on a slight incline, I jumped off the machine and took a moment to steady myself. Treadmills always had a tendency to throw my equilibrium off a bit, but usually only for a moment or two. Then I walked upstairs and jumped into the shower where I began to mentally prepare for my day. Under the cool water, I washed away most of my worries from the day before. Today, I had work to do. That would occupy my time for the better part of the day and allow me to step back and clear my head. Later I would chat with Thomas and ask about the photos, but for now, it could wait.

After supper, I found Thomas waiting for me online as usual. We had a standing cyber date most evenings. After we exchanged the usual pleasantries about each other's day, I decided to gingerly inch my way into my inquiries and, as a true lady, I tried my diplomatic hand at subtlety.

"Is that really you in those photos? They look like they were taken professionally of a model."

I was never very good at subtlety.

Thomas did not respond right away.

Did I insult him? Damn. I should really learn how to be a bit more tactful, I thought, but Thomas seemed to take it all in stride.

"Of course they are of me. Who else? A friend took them. He is a trained photographer. Professional model, you say? I think I am quite flattered."

"Well, they look wonderful. Perhaps you missed your calling," I typed.

"I can assure you he used a lot of lenses and filters. I am afraid it was all in the photography."

"I think you underestimate your appearance, Thomas."

"Thank you."

I resigned myself to the fact he must be telling me the truth. Every time I had a quandary, he made sense of it. Every time I questioned something, he responded with logic. I was beginning to feel like a drama queen.

When we logged off, I thought about a few other things that helped alleviate some of my misgivings. First, I was a journalist – a journalist who was used to people lying to her. I questioned everything and doubted everyone. Cynicism was part of the gig. Second, I told myself I could not tell what a person's voice sounded like by simply seeing them in a photo. That was purely laughable. Third, I concluded the doubts Marianne had planted about meeting someone over the Internet were starting to make me suspicious of everything. I decided to give him the benefit of the doubt. Realistically, all I really had were suspicions, not proof. It took me a long time, but I now believed not all people had a hidden agenda and there were still good, honest people in this god-forsaken world of ours. I had to. It took me far to long to finally have faith in that notion.

CHAPTER 6

The next few weeks were truly defining chapters in mine and Thomas's relationship. I had finally let go of most of my preliminary uncertainties, and Thomas started to open up quite a bit more. Our telephone calls were still very limited, but our e-mails became much more personal, and I found out, Thomas, truly was a romantic.

One morning, I went online to check my e-mails and found one from him. It was dated 3:42 a.m. that morning and simply read:

A Magic Moment I Remember – Pushkin
A magic moment I remember:
I raised my eyes and you were there,
A fleeting vision, the quintessence
Of all that's beautiful and rare.
I pray to mute despair and anguish,
To vain pursuits the world esteems,
Long did I near your soothing accents,
Long did your features haunt my dreams.
Time passed. A rebel storm-blast scattered
The reveries that once were mine
And I forgot your soothing accents,
Your features gracefully divine.
In dark days of enforced retirement
I gazed upon grey skies above
With no ideals to inspire me,
No one to cry for, live for, love.
Then came a moment of renaissance,
I looked up - you again are there,
A fleeting vision, the quintessence
Of all that's beautiful and rare.

At first, it was very strange to me, feeling this close to someone I had never even met, especially from a romantic perspective. In fact, up until a few weeks ago, I never would have thought it possible. But there I was right in the middle of it and feeling like the whole thing was perfectly natural. I knew Thomas must have felt the same way. He seemed to open up to me about everything now. Then one day, his e-mail took on a slightly different tone. I received a rather long e-mail regarding his feelings about where he was and what he was seeing. I knew how he felt, although my job never really put me in the same kind of danger he was in.

Realities, especially the realities of war, were cold and harsh and bitter. Reading about war and living through it were two totally dissimilar things. As a society, we had become quite desensitized to the atrocities of war; and, while most of us agreed it was all 'very sad', we never truly gave it in-depth or detailed thought. And, like anyone seeing carnage day in and day out, the effects of war can never truly be erased from someone's mind. Thomas too had his limitations, but I was very pleased he felt comfortable enough to share his thoughts with me. Sometimes I too found it very hard to take my emotions out of a story. I could only imagine what Thomas must have felt being there during an actual war.

Hello Bella.

Thank you for spending so many hours chatting with me and although you are not aware, taking my mind off most things happening here. I choose to do this in an e-mail rather than online for fear of disrupting our very special moments.

I do not profess to know what is happening across the border in Israel, as I am not there to witness it directly, but I am sure there will be the same heartache there as here in Beirut. The deadly fighting between Israel and Hezbollah has taken its toll on so many people, but my heart aches for the children. All the children.

I cannot imagine living as any of these children do. They are in such constant fear of air strikes, car bombings, and land mines, that they cannot help but treat it as part of a normal life. It is so very sad to know this 'acceptance,' for lack of a better term, is truly just an intrinsic part of a human being's survival instinct. I see brave faces everywhere, yet their eyes deceive them. I can only hope one day their world will be at peace. No child should ever have to live in fear. The desensitization they have endured is inhuman; yet, they still hold on to unwavering dreams for the future. Sometimes I feel so very lucky to be born where I was and given the opportunities I was; yet, I cannot help but think the only reason I grew up in England, as opposed to here, is all just because of an accident of birth. Where we are born and who we are born to is all out of our hands, is it not?

It also frustrates me to know the Western media is currently focusing their attention on a recent Hollywood marriage scandal as opposed to the kidnapped Israeli soldiers who are still missing. I will never understand the world's fanaticism with Hollywood's negative gossip instead of current humanitarian tragedies, but I digress.

Since the cease fire, I have watched as some of the local schools are being rebuilt and this is a good thing. I have stood on the construction sites and closed my eyes and imagined the sounds of children's laughter once again echoing through the playground. It is a wonderful sound in my head, so I hold on to it tightly.

Sometimes when my colleagues and I go to the local café in the evenings, we try to make sense of it all by trying to analyse the rationale behind the philosophy of war. Yet, we all still come to the same conclusion – as long as there is a

thirst for supremacy, whether through money, land, religion or plain ignorance, there will always be war. If I have depressed you, I sincerely apologise. I hope I will see brighter and happier things in the days to come that will give me fresh hope in humanity and cause me to write in happier tones. With time, I will. But, please, just do not ask me now.
Thomas

I was happy Thomas felt he could open up to me. And, although our relationship sounded more like fiction than real life, he was as authentic to me as any other person in my life. Any reservations I still had about Thomas now lingered in the back of my mind and not in the forefront. At times I questioned whether I was being realistic by doing so; but, I desperately wanted to give him the benefit of the doubt. Besides, I was too caught up in the whirlwind of it all now to give those uncertainties as much validity as I once had.

CHAPTER 7

While I stood in the confines of my kitchen pantry wondering what to make for lunch, I heard that familiar New Orleans's funeral march and made my way downstairs to answer the door. It was Marianne.

"Hello, stranger," she said sarcastically.

"Hello," I replied, with a little grin not wanting to take the bait. "I was just about to make some lunch. Would you care to join me?"

"Actually, I'm famished. What's on the menu?" she asked, as she took off her sling-back heels and sauntered her way barefoot up the foyer stairs and towards the kitchen.

I fell in step behind her. "I was just deciding when you rang. What do you feel like?"

"How about a nice chicken Caesar salad, some caramel coffee cake and a big dollop of juicy gossip to go on top of it?"

"Subtle. Very subtle."

"Well, you are the one who's disappeared for the last month," she said, as she sat down on one of the kitchen bar stools next to the pantry.

"I have been working on that analysis, remember?"

"So it's done then?"

"Not quite."

"What do you mean, not quite?"

"I mean it's not quite done yet."

"How much longer do you need?"

"I don't know, another few weeks."

"A few weeks? What the hell have you been doing? This is elementary for a seasoned professional like you."

"I've been distracted," I said, trying not to make direct eye contact with her.

Only after a brief hesitation, Marianne said, "You've met someone!"

"Maybe."

"Maybe, my eye. That's like saying you kind of slept with someone. Either you have or you haven't, now which is it?"

"Okay, I've met someone," I said, with diaphanous self-confidence.

"You mean in person, right?" Marianne ventured cautiously.

"No. I mean I've met someone. He's too far away to meet with just yet."

"Hmmm," Marianne said, looking at me and shaking her head.

"What? He's a gorgeous surgeon volunteering in Lebanon."

Marianne laughed. "Yeah, and George Clooney might be popping over for cocktails later, naked, with his pot-bellied pig in tow."

"Very funny. Okay, so he sounds too good to be true. Doesn't mean he's a fraud."

"I never once said he was a fraud. Was that a Freudian slip?"

"No. It wasn't," I said defensively. "I really have had some great conversations with this guy."

"How do you even know he is who he says he is? Anyone can say anything online. Cyberspace breeds fantasy, my dear."

"Look you cynic. Leave me to my little online fling. I'm enjoying it. Besides, this one kind of caught me off guard."

"Really?" she said, as she raised one eyebrow at me. "All right, it's your life. What's his name anyway?"

"It's Thomas."

Marianne let out a huge laugh.

"Why are you laughing? It's a very distinguished name."

"Do you know what the synonym for cynic is?" she asked.

"No enlighten me," I said sarcastically, as I walked past her on my way to the fridge.

"It's a Doubting Thomas," she said, and started to laugh again.

"Very funny. Who the hell are you, Ellen DeGeneres?"

I don't know why I got so defensive. Was I truly mad at Marianne's cynicism, or did she hit a nerve? One way or the other, I was bound to prove her wrong. I was too proud not to. Besides, I think she really did hit a nerve.

That night, when Thomas contacted me, I figured I would test the foundation of Marianne's disparagements and suggest we meet. Dreading how he might respond, I waited patiently for his answer. I was pleasantly surprised, as he met the idea with enthusiasm and excitement.

"You read my mind. I just found out today I can leave whenever I wish. My tour is over; but, I did not want to say anything, just in case they needed me to stay on. Another surgeon arrived today to take my place. I was going to broach the subject with you tonight as a matter of fact."

"Really? That is very nice to hear," I typed, feeling quite relieved.

"Now it is just a matter of the particulars. When and where?" he asked.

Feeling some of Marianne's self-inflicting doubt sweep away from me, we delved into our plans to meet. I don't know why I acted so impulsively, considering I had loads of work to do and a not-so-patient editor, but I did, and agreed to meet with him the following week. He was on his way back to England to see his family, and I agreed to join him there.

"I cannot wait. Now we can finally do this properly. In person. Face to face."

"Yes," I replied. "This has truly been a very interesting experience for me, but I agree wholeheartedly. We need to meet face to face."

"I will book the flight. Do not worry about a thing. I will e-mail you the itinerary as soon as it is confirmed," he typed.

"You don't have to do that, Thomas."

"I do not wish for you to worry about one thing. Please, I would like to do this."

"Thank you," I typed.

"It is my pleasure. I will see you the beginning of next week."

"Yes, you will. I'd better go. I'll have to organize a few things before I can leave."

"I understand," he typed. "Take care."

"Yes, you too," I replied, then I logged off.

At last, this entire internal struggle of mine was finally going to end. Now, I could get to know this brilliant-minded person and stop over-analysing the whole situation. I felt such a sense of relief. He wasn't trying to hide anything at all. I was just being paranoid.

I stood up and began to make a mental list of all the things I had to do before I left, one of which was to call Marianne.

CHAPTER 8

The days flew by quickly, mostly because I had a lot of work to catch up on. It was arduous, but worth it. After that, I only had the simpler things to look after. I asked Mrs. Goldman to look after my plants, something she did every time I went away. I didn't bother with the cleaning services because I wasn't going to be gone long enough to warrant them. I exchanged some currency and put my mail on hold at the post office. It was all falling into place. Even my boss was agreeable to me leaving on such short notice because his nephew was keen on filling my shoes for a bit, something I was also very grateful for.

It was just before midnight on Sunday night and I sat staring out the glass doors of my living room watching a small sliver of brushed bronze moon glide over the escarpment. Again, I could not believe how quickly the last few days had gone by. My bags were packed, and I was waiting for a taxi to come and take me to the airport. I always chose the red eye. Less pandemonium.

I lifted my teacup to my lips and noticed my hands were a bit shaky. Despite the fact I had been communicating with Thomas quite a bit over the last month or so, I still didn't really know what to expect. At first, I was quite excited to finally be meeting him, but now I was getting nervous. I don't know why, but I was starting to get that niggling feeling in the pit of my stomach again. I told myself I was just over analysing things. Surely, it must just be nerves, I thought. Well, it was either nerves over meeting Thomas, or nerves over the fact that I told Marianne where I was going in an e-mail, instead of over the phone. I was such a coward, but I knew what her reaction would be. She was going to have kittens over this one. I guess I just couldn't face listening to all the pessimistic dialogue again. I was nervous enough. If I had to endure yet another one of her diatribes about the pitfalls of online dating, I would be too rattled to enjoy myself.

The door chime began to sing and I nearly jumped out of my skin.

"Stop it, Frankie," I said aloud. "This is going to be either the most exciting adventure of your life or the biggest mistake in female history. Either way, it'll be one hell of a ride."

I checked to see that the stove was off. Perhaps one day I will invest in a proper kettle instead of using a pot to boil water. I grabbed my luggage and put my teacup in the sink – there is never an excuse for being untidy. Then I made my way downstairs and into the brightly lit yellow taxi that was waiting for me.

"To *zee* airport and step on it," I said, doing my finest Inspector Clouseau impression.

No response.

I shrugged. Everyone's a critic.

CHAPTER 9

Terminal three at Lester B. Pearson airport was crowded, despite the hour. As requested, I arrived three hours in advance, stood in an insanely long line and argued with a woman from airport security when she refused to let me bring my hairspray or perfume onboard in my carry-on luggage.

"How am I supposed to make a dazzling entrance into Gatwick airport without my essentials?" I asked.

After several moments discussing the issue, and several more admonitions regarding national security from her, I concluded she had no sense of humour and wasn't about to budge; so, I turned on my heel and marched through the second set of doors towards Gate 7, *sans* my hairspray and perfume and wondering where her entourage of flying monkeys were.

Once the plane took off, I had more time to ponder this whole expedition of mine. In fact, I had seven hours to ponder it. So, I made myself as comfortable as I could, drank two glasses of Folonari Valpolicella, ate a rather nice meal of stuffed chicken, garden salad and scones with clotted cream, and decided to recline my seat to mull things over.

Okay, so I've had some doubts. It obviously came with the territory. We met online and everything about dating has to change when you meet someone that way. I mean, there are so many variables to consider. It is much easier in person because you can always rely on common sense, chemistry, voice inflection. That holds true with photos as well, I rationalized. I've had dozens of photos taken of me that look nothing like me – most of which I had to burn. It's a vanity thing. So, until technology invents a three dimensional way to enhance people in one dimensional photos, we are stuck with mere baseline replicas of each other. The bottom line here is I have been over analysing this whole situation because there have just been too many variables to think about. In another few hours, all questions will be laid to rest and I can spend the next week or so getting to know Thomas. I mean it was perfectly natural to have doubts. I am sure Thomas must be feeling the same way I was. Perhaps we shall even share a laugh over it.

I finally fell asleep during the last few hours of my journey and woke to the familiar chimes indicating all passengers to fasten their seatbelts. There was also an announcement saying we were circling Gatwick airport, the current temperature was 23° Celsius and it was 3:20 p.m. local time, five hours later than my watch read. The voice also thanked us for flying with them and welcomed us to England.

After everyone disembarked the plane, we all began making our way towards the baggage claim area. The airport was crowded but the signs were fairly easy to follow. Baggage claim was just up ahead and to my right.

I stood there watching the bags make their way down the ramp and onto the conveyor belt. My bag was among the first load to come down the ramp. As I grabbed for it, the damn thing almost took me with it. I had no idea why they had the conveyor belt at such a high speed. It was probably set up like that on purpose, I thought. At this very moment, there were probably half a dozen security guards watching us through the security cameras, drinking coffee and having a good laugh over the whole thing.

Getting through customs went rather smoothly. I expected to have at least a bit of a delay with the recent arrests in London of twenty-four alleged terrorists who were planning an attack on American soil. Apparently, British authorities foiled a plot that was supposed to emulate September 11, 2001.

It's a new world now, I thought. Everyone was limited to what they could bring onboard in their carry-on luggage. All items purchased at airports were now being toted around in clear plastic bags, even the rubbish bins at all the bus depots and airports were lined with clear plastic bags. I began to wonder what the world would be like in another ten, twenty or even fifty years. Would there be another world war? Would humans ultimately destroy each other and the planet they lived on because of different belief systems? Would it ever be possible to have such a vast population of people live in harmony? Would the ruling world powers be able to remain unchanged without nuclear involvement? Are we perhaps only one miscalculation away from total annihilation?

As I slowly made my way towards the arrival area, my mind still deep in thought, someone tapped me on the shoulder and I jumped. Actually, I didn't just jump; I think I did air time. One day, my preoccupations were going to get me hurt, I thought. One day, I'll probably walk right off a curb and into a bus.

I turned around nervously, expecting to see Thomas standing there, but instead, it was a porter. For some reason, he just stood there staring at me. I didn't know whether he was staring because he assumed I knew what he wanted, or because he was impressed at how high I could jump on such short notice. Either way, I still thought I should say something.

"Sorry. You startled me," I said. Original, I thought, but it was all I could come up with on short notice. Perhaps the next time I'll try an amphibian anecdote.

He was a rather stout man, with no neck, and a uniform jacket that looked entirely unsuited for his shape. He smiled cordially and finally asked if I needed any help with my bags.

I politely declined and made my way out the South Terminal gates and into the main reception area. As I made my way through the crowd, I looked around at all the people hugging, laughing, and obviously happy to see whomever it was they were greeting. I recognized several accents of Scottish decent, several English ones, and a few that were barely discernable – probably Welsh, I thought. That language always amazed me. I remembered a professor I had at university. She was from Swansea. I asked her once, out of sheer curiosity, how someone would say "Nice to meet you" in Welsh.

She replied, "'n glws at chwrdd 'ch."

She wasn't joking.

I continued to look around. Everyone seemed to be finding exactly whom he or she was supposed to, but there was no single entity looking around waiting for me.

As the crowd began to thin, I thought perhaps I had passed Thomas en route so I doubled back towards the baggage claim. Nothing. After twenty minutes of searching, I decided it was better to stay in one place just in case he was doing the same thing I was. I found a railing outside the baggage claim area, just inside the nearest exit doors, and propped myself up against it. Looking around, I noticed only one gentleman by himself. He glanced over at me, but I immediately dismissed him as being Thomas because he was blonde and slender. Thomas was tall, dark and brawny. Several minutes and several glances later, I was wondering if he thought he knew me, but then someone else tapped me on the shoulder and I felt a rush of excitement. I turned around and found a woman standing in front of me, wearing an airline uniform and holding a small envelope.

"Are you Francesca Bradford?" she asked.

"Yes. Is that for me?" I asked, looking down at her hand.

"Yes," she replied. "I took this message about half an hour ago. I'm sorry it took me this long to find you, but we have been very busy with these last flights that have just come in."

"That's fine," I said, and took the envelope from her. "Thank you."

My heart raced as I stared down at the white envelope. I looked around one more time and noticed my blonde admirer was now making his way towards the exit doors and chatting on his mobile phone. Strange, I thought. He never left with anyone.

Before opening the note, I made my way to a specialty coffee house, just across from Harrods. I ordered a decaf latté with cinnamon sprinkled on the top, sat down and leaned the note up against the sugar container to stare at it.

What if he wasn't coming? I thought. What if Marianne was right and this was a huge mistake? I took a sip of my coffee, burning my tongue in the process. I hated that sensation. It always left that awful spongy feeling on my tongue for days.

Then I began to mull over my situation. What if he didn't show? Why would I take that so personally anyway? I was getting defensive now. If he backed out, it was not a reflection on me. He was the fool – okay, I had to stop watching Dr. Phil.

I sipped my latté for two more minutes, licked some of the cinnamon from my upper lip, and thought I might as well get it over with. That way I could still figure out a way to salvage the two weeks of vacation I had just booked at the last minute. So on that conjecture, I gently tore open the tiny envelope and read the note inside.

Frankie,

Please forgive me but I am unable to meet you in Gatwick. Please go to the Fairbanks Inn on High Street in Hythe, Kent. I have booked us a room under the name of Bradford. I will meet you there. I will explain everything when I see you.

Thomas

CHAPTER 10

I looked around. Nothing was amiss. There were no cameras, no grips, no stage crew, and no directors yelling, "Cut!" This was getting ridiculous. Who the hell was I meeting, Thomas Bissett or James Bond?

After I finished my latté, I made my way back to the main concourse, walked outside, and hailed a taxi. What the hell was Thomas playing at? I asked myself. I hopped into the backseat of the cab and informed the driver where I had to go. He looked at me through his rear view mirror and informed me Hythe was just better than an hour from the airport.

"Are you sure that's where you want to go?" he questioned, in a very thick East-London accent.

I re-read Thomas's note and confirmed our destination. Then, we drove out of the airport and made our way onto the A23. From there, we drove for a bit then merged onto the M23. After that I saw some signs for Dartford and Sevenoaks; but, I wasn't really paying too much attention to them. I was still trying to get my head wrapped around the fact Thomas didn't meet me at the airport and he was making me travel over an hour to some hotel in a town I'd never even heard of. He mentioned his family lived in Paddington, in west central London. So why was he redirecting me here? I wondered. I was starting to get a headache with all the information whirling around in my head; so, I decided to just sit back, relax and wait until Thomas could explain everything.

Driving down the highway and looking around helped to keep my mind occupied, but just barely. I had always wanted to come to the United Kingdom, so my five senses were working overtime as I took everything in. It was always strange to me seeing everything on the opposite side of the motorway. I had now been to three countries where that was the norm, but it still took some getting used to.

One of the most striking features that jumped out at me here was the fact that everything seemed so enduring, so steeped in history. Canada was not quite one hundred and forty years old, a comparative stripling to the UK. But then again I guess it would seem that way. The UK had been inhabited for thousands of years before Canada was.

We were about three quarters of an hour into our journey when we passed a sign that immediately caught my attention. It read, 'Canterbury.'

"I never knew we'd be passing Canterbury," I said excitedly, to the driver. "I love Jeffrey Chaucer."

I think I startled him a bit. We had barely said half a dozen words to each other the whole trip.

"Indeed," he replied.

"I wrote a paper on the Neolithic finds at Canterbury as an undergrad," I said.

"Did you," he said. "And what was your major?"

"Journalism," I said. "But I took loads of anthropology courses during my first two years."

"And what is anthropology, exactly?" he asked, glancing at me intermittently through his rear view mirror.

I laughed a little and said, "You have no idea how many people ask me that question. It's a bit of an all-encompassing term because it is such a vast discipline," I explained. "It is broken down into a lot of different categories like, Physical Anthropology, Cultural Anthropology, Forensic Anthropology, Archaeology…"

"Ah, like Indiana Jones," he said.

I let that one go.

"I guess the best way to describe it is to say that it encompasses all of humanity over all timelines and in all dimensions. For example, did you know that there was evidence of Homo erectus found here in Norfolk and Suffolk that dates back 700,000 years?" I offered, hoping it would provide him with a better understanding.

He smiled, remotely feigning interest, and said, "Sounds, umm, interesting."

I caught the vague expression on his face through the rear view mirror and decided to let him off the hook.

"So tell me more about Canterbury," I said.

"Usually people want to hear about the murder of Thomas Becket," he said, a lilt of interest now creeping back into his voice.

"He was the archbishop at Canterbury Cathedral, wasn't he?" I asked, hoping I was remembering my history correctly.

"That's right. He was murdered by King Henry II. Well, he gave the orders anyway. Did you study British history as well?" he asked.

"I read a lot. I don't have much of a social life," I said jokingly.

Then reality set in and the laughing subsided as I remembered that my 'social life' was now only minutes away from me, or at least with any luck he would be.

"Thank you," I said, brushing a stray hair off my forehead and leaning back in my seat again.

"For what, Miss?" he asked, furrowing his salt and pepper brow.

"For the distraction," I said, smiling. "It was much needed."

When we finally arrived, I stepped out of the cab and onto the cobblestone streets of Hythe. The sun was shining and High Street was bustling with activity. What a charming place, I thought. Hythe was indeed magnificent – Medieval and Georgian buildings steeped in history with loads of picturesque little shops to browse through. Perhaps this was all going to work out after all, I thought. Nothing alleviates anxiety like retail therapy.

Once I had gathered my bags and took several deep breaths of sea air, I paid my driver £60 and looked down a small path and saw the sign for the Fairbanks Inn. I began making my way down the path towards the entrance of the inn, trying desperately to ignore the butterflies in the hollow of my stomach.

As I stepped inside the front door, I noticed the Fairbanks Inn was more like a bed and breakfast than an actual inn. The main reception area was rather quaint and coloured in ornate reds and browns. The sparse furniture consisted of two Georgian rope-back chairs, which were covered with a delicate paisley print, a coffee table and two Tiffany-style lamps. There was also a solid-oak bureau that doubled as a reception table and housed several black and white photos of an elderly couple looking rather grim, or at least not too pleased to be having their photo taken. I wondered why every black and white photo I had ever seen was taken of people who never smiled.

Off to the left, in an adjoining room, was a very sturdy-looking dining room table that was draped in crisp white linen. There were four settings for tea on it, which were all untouched. There was also a hint of lavender in the air, probably from little sachets placed in dresser drawers. My grandmother always used to do that. Some scents have the most incredible way of bringing back wonderful memories. She had been gone for almost six years now, and I missed her terribly. Perhaps I could convince Thomas to take me up to Glasgow for a couple of days. I'd love to find the house she was born in.

I heard a door open somewhere near the back of the inn and a moment later I saw the door in front of me open. In walked a frail-looking woman with grey hair and a sparkle in her eye. She walked towards me, while wiping her hands on her blue and white striped pinny and gave me a very welcoming smile. She introduced herself as Minnie Simpson, the owner of the inn. I shook her still-damp hand and introduced myself. She lifted her finger as if she was remembering something and walked over to the guest book that was lying on the top of the bureau.

"Yes," she said. "We have been expecting you, Ms. Bradford."

"Frankie, please," I said, as I placed my hand on my chest.

She looked up, smiled, and said, "Of course."

She had one of the loveliest Scottish accents I had ever heard. I loved the way the Scots rolled their 'r's.

"Mr. Bissett made sure we saved a very lovely room for the two of you. I am sure you will like it," she said, again with the sparkle in her eye. Perhaps that was a trick only the British knew how to perform.

"Has Mr. Bissett arrived yet?" I dared to venture.

"Oh, yes indeed. He's waiting for you upstairs," she said, smiling.

I think my heart skipped a beat just then. All this running around in somewhat controlled chaos had finally come to an end. He was here.

"Follow me," she said. "Just leave your bags where they are for now and I'll get William to bring them up in a bit."

We walked up a very steep set of red-carpeted stairs that were also a bit uneven and creaked as we made our way to the top. The banister smelled of freshly applied lemon-scented wood oil. When we reached the first landing, she turned and handed me a key on a long gold chain that also held a round clasp with the inn's initials embossed on it.

"If you would like something to eat, I can have a tray brought up," she offered.

"Thank you," I said, twiddling the chain around my fingers. "That is most appreciated. We'll let you know."

She patted my arm and ventured back down the stairs humming almost inaudibly to herself.

I stood staring at the door for a few seconds, took in a deep breath and put the key in the lock. The lock opened with ease, but the door creaked as much as the stairs did. I walked into the room and let the door slowly close behind me. The thick curtains were closed and there were candles lit ubiquitously around the room. I also heard the voice of some soft crooning male singer I did not recognize delicately wafting out of a radio in the corner of the room. Again, I smelled the lavender, but it was much stronger now. I also heard the faint sound of running water coming from the bathroom. I waited, unable to move another step without shaking and then I heard the water shut off. I just stood there waiting for the bathroom door to eventually open up. When it finally did, out stepped a man I did not recognize.

CHAPTER 11

"Frankie," the man said, as he started walking towards me wearing only a stark white hotel towel wrapped around his waist. Apparently modesty wasn't an issue.

As he walked closer and my eyes began to focus in the dimness of the candle-lit room, I began to recognize the face, but not entirely.

"Thomas?" I asked hesitantly "You look so different."

"Not really," Thomas said, with an unrecognizable low-pitched chuckle.

It was definitely not the same voice I heard on the phone.

He slowly approached me, his eyes fixed on mine. He did not even blink. He took my hands, raised them both to his lips and kissed them. He smelled of good aftershave, or cologne, Hugo Boss, I think, and still had drops of moisture on his cheeks and brow. He stood there staring at me for what seemed like an eternity, then he let my hands drop and slowly backed away slightly shaking his head back and forth. I watched him carefully as he backed away. It was true. He did look somewhat like the photos he sent me, but his dark wavy hair was now highlighted and cut shorter. His ultra-thin goatee was gone, replaced with what must have been an ever-present five o'clock shadow, and were those contacts he was wearing?

"You are even more beautiful in person. I cannot believe you are finally here."

"Speaking of here, why did you not meet me in Gatwick?" I asked, trying to disregard the unfamiliarity of his voice.

"Come. Freshen up first, then we will go find something to eat and I will explain everything to you."

I decided to take Thomas up on his offer and made my way to the bathroom to clear my head. I stepped into the sterile-looking bathroom of white and chrome, splashed some very cold water on my face and looked up into the mirror. He just wasn't the Thomas I was expecting to find, I thought. Okay, so he did resemble the photos, but that voice! Was it possible to have such a variation in voice over bad phone lines? I mean, we did only speak by telephone on a few occasions, I rationalized. Mostly, we communicated through e-mails and instant messaging. I guess the only thing that gave me a fairly decent amount of comfort was the fact that his accent and expressions were pretty much the same. I wanted to say something, but I knew it was probably going to come out sounding ridiculous. Was I just being paranoid again?

Twenty minutes later, we were on our way down the tiny staircase, past the front rooms and out into the early-evening air. I took several more deep breaths as soon as we stepped outside. The salty air was cool and refreshing, a great improvement to what I had just left behind in Ontario. I felt new life being infused into me.

"What a beautiful evening," I said, looking towards the sky. "This is what my grandmother used to call the gloaming hour – that magical hour, right before sunset, when the scents of the flowers were at their strongest."

"I have heard that," he said. "And, yes, it is a magnificent evening."

There was also a calm about Hythe, and I felt myself starting to relax a bit.

The streets of Hythe were more or less empty now. Most of the shops were closed and the only din that could be heard was coming from a pub down the street and to the left. I let Thomas guide us to our destination as we walked in silence, which was most welcome as it gave me some time to gather my thoughts. I took everything in as we eventually made our way past the pub, through a back alleyway, across a main thoroughfare, and eventually along a path that led down the side of a canal. The trees that lined the canal must have been hundreds of years old; the tips of their long willowy branches dipping slightly into the water. There were people in rowboats going up and down the canal, couples mostly, and the ducks were wading through them like they didn't have a care in the world.

As we walked over the bridge, Thomas was the first one to break the silence.

"This canal was built to keep Napoleon out, and just over there is the English Channel," he said, pointing to his left.

"So this is not your first time here?" I asked.

"Yes, it is, but I arrived yesterday so I have already had the chance to look around," he said, still smiling.

He always seemed to be smiling. It was such a refreshing change. The world seemed to be filled with a lot more curmudgeons than optimists these days.

"Why didn't you meet me in Gatwick? I assumed you weren't even in England yet and that is why you were delayed."

"All in good time, Bella. Ah, here is the ristorante," he said.

Ristorante? Bella? His accent was not Italian. In fact, his accent was not discernable to me at all. It was definitely European, but from where? And his last name. It was Bissett. French? His accent was not French either. I was just about to say something, but I decided to take in a deep breath instead. Then I reminded myself I was not Nancy Drew and he was not a suspect. I told myself not to ask too many questions all at once, to keep it simple, and to remember we had the next two weeks ahead of us. There was plenty of time to talk.

It was hard for me not to do that, not to ask questions. I felt as if I didn't trust anyone half the time. My job didn't help, of course. People lied to me all the time. I was used to it. Unfortunately, that only contributed to my doubt sometimes, but there was another major contributing factor that led to that distrust. It was all because of Józef, but I didn't want to venture there again. Not right now. Let it go Frankie, I told myself quickly. That was a very long time ago.

I suddenly realized Thomas was saying something to me.

"Pardon?" I said.

"Are you all right?" He turned to look at me.

"Yes, of course, sorry, I was just thinking about something."

"So, do you like it?"

I looked up to see an extraordinary old dwelling, undeniably 17th or 18th century, that had been converted into a restaurant. It simply oozed charm – Palladian charm. The architecture was exquisite and absolutely definable, from the colonnades and Roman accents to the vast portico and low mezzanine. Yes. It was definitely Palladian.

"Oh, Thomas," I beamed. "It is absolutely brilliant. The architecture is incredible."

"I knew you would like it," he said, as he smiled. Then he took my hand and led me into the restaurant. As we made our way through the front doors, aromas of Far East spices wafted into my nose and made my mouth water. I breathed deeper. The air was so thick with scents they seemed to hover in mid air enticing our senses even more as we waded through them. The main room was quite dim. Little lamps strategically placed on circular tables seemed to be the only source of lighting. It was not too crowded, half a dozen well-dressed patrons at the most, but then again we were dining rather early, even by English standards.

Thomas placed his hand on my lower back and led me into a small waiting area off to our left-hand side. There were only six chairs, surrounding three end tables, and a tiny coat check room. Thomas gestured for me to sit down, kissed the back of my hand, excused himself and walked down the hallway to the left. Not five minutes later, a waiter appeared with a glass of red wine for me. I took a large sip, let out an audible sigh, and thanked him. It was my Wolf Blass. How refreshing it was to have a man remember all the little things you mention in passing. I was starting to relax even more and feeling very spoiled all at the same time. I sat back and snuggled into the soft stuffing of the chair. I put my feet up on the foot stool and took another rather large gulp of wine. The warmth of the deep burgundy liquid seemed to wrap itself around me, and I could feel the stresses of the day physically leaving my body. A few minutes later, Thomas appeared. He took one look at me, leaned up against the doorframe and smiled.

"You look the vision of tranquillity," he said.

I grinned back at him.

"Come, our table is ready," he said, extending his arm for me to take.

We walked past the main dining area, through a set of French doors, up a flight of stairs and onto the rooftop. There, waiting for us was the most magnificent table set for two, complete with candles, wine, soft music, and as I looked to my left, that final ribbon of red sun that was slowly slipping down behind the water.

I looked at Thomas and smiled.

"As promised," he said, grinning.

Dinner was utterly delectable. We started with sautéed foie gras served with peach chutney. The main course was roasted sea bass with chive crème fraiche, baby potatoes and artichoke, followed by panacotta with marinated raspberries for desert. The dinner conversation was equally delicious. We spoke of education, politics, photography, architecture and several other topics of mutual interest. In fact, I couldn't remember the last time I spoke with someone who completely swaddled me in such stimulating intellect as much as Thomas did. No subject was untouchable, no topic proscribed. I thought very briefly about some of my unanswered questions as to his whereabouts, but quickly dismissed them as not to spoil the mood or the rest of the evening. Tonight was just about the two of us, here, now. I wasn't about to complicate it. I found it very easy to be with him. I had all along, even through our long-distance dialogues. When you are with someone who makes you feel like this, it is very easy to dismiss doubts, I thought.

After dinner, we strolled out of the restaurant and down to the waterfront. Several people were strolling along the boardwalk as well. The moon was low in the sky and reflecting off the water. The sound of the ocean rolled in and with it the magnificent scent of salt air. It made everything seem more real to me. It was everything we talked about, everything we said we were looking forward to, and now, it was tangible.

As we made our way down the stretch of beach to a place called Sandgate, I snuggled in closer to Thomas as he wrapped his arm around me and kissed me on the top of my head. I felt as if I had known him a lot longer than just over a month.

Then he stopped, turned around to face me, bent his head down and kissed me. He lifted his lips from mine, smiled at me, sighed, and turned us around to walk back in the direction of the inn.

The last time I remember looking at the clock, it was 4:53 a.m.

CHAPTER 12

The next morning, I awoke to the vague scent of Thomas's cologne on my pillow and a note that read: *Back soon. T. xxoo.*

Probably gone to get something for breakfast, I thought. I got up, scrubbed my face, brushed my teeth, swallowed about a litre of water, put on my running gear and set out. I was in desperate need of my four kilometre run. I was a bit tired and I knew I would be totally ineffective mentally, and physically, for the rest of the day without it. I decided to head towards the beachfront and figured I could be back before Thomas even noticed me gone.

The seaside was filled with people fishing, people walking, kids splashing and seniors sitting on the freshly painted benches that were dotted along the English Channel coastline. The sun was shining, and I found a renewed energy as I weaved my way in and out of the people around me.

As I made my way around the winding path, my mind deep in thought about last night, I glanced up and noticed someone leaning over the dividing wall watching me. I did a double-take, and the man who seemed to be watching me swiftly turned to face the buildings on the other side of the roadway. My heart stopped for an instant. My head was racing. Was he the blonde man I saw at Gatwick airport? I stopped running, turned, and began walking briskly towards him. I had no idea what I was going to say to him, but I had to talk to him. I had to know why he was there and why he seemed to have such an interest in me. Perhaps it was all just a coincidence and I was about to make a colossal fool out of myself, but I still had to know.

I had only made it a few paces up the first stone-covered mound, the ones that separated the path from the dividing wall, when a dark grey sedan pulled up in front of him. Two men got out of the car, grabbed the man by both arms and forcefully pushed him into the backseat of the car. A split second later, they sped off in the direction of Sandgate.

I stopped dead in my tracks. I couldn't move. My breathing was even more laboured than when I was running. I just stood there staring at the spot where the man once stood not a few seconds ago. What the hell was going on? I don't know how long it was before I finally gathered my senses and began to make my way back to the inn, but on the way back I began hoping and praying Thomas would be there.

CHAPTER 13

From the other side of the road, slightly down the beach, a mobile phone rang.
"Yes?"
"Were you watching?" the voice asked.
"Yes," Thomas said.
"How close were you?"
"Less than twenty metres. I never took my eyes off her."
"Does she know him?" the voice asked.
"Yes, I think she does," Thomas said.
"It is very important we gauge her reaction accurately," the voice said, sounding quite adamant. "You know what is at stake here."
"After she spotted him, she began walking towards him," Thomas said. "Our car arrived just in time, but she did not look pleasantly surprised to see him. She looked visibly perplexed. This is not what we expected. I have to go. She is heading back towards the inn, probably looking for me. I will be in touch as soon as I have talked with her."
"Remember, do not underestimate her," the voice cautioned.
"Do not worry," Thomas said, then he hung up and walked quickly back to his car.

CHAPTER 14

As I made my way up the stairs to our room, I began to feel dizzy; so, I stopped for a moment at the top of the landing and tried to compose myself before unlocking the door and stepping inside. Even though I was rather troubled by what I had just witnessed, I still didn't want to come across as sounding totally daft.

I opened the door and found Thomas sitting in one of the burgundy winged-backed chairs reading what I suspected to be the local newspaper. He lowered the paper, took one look at me and said, "Frankie, what is wrong? You look upset."

"Thomas," I stammered, then quickly tried to regain my voice. "Something happened. I just went for a run on the beach, and I saw a man staring at me. At least I think he was staring at me. He was the same man I saw at the airport when I was waiting for you. I think he followed me here."

Thomas stood up, walked over to me, placed his hands on my shoulders, looked into my eyes and said, "What same man? And why would anyone be following you?"

I stood motionless for a moment, staring back at him. "I don't know," I said, shaking my head trying to gather my thoughts.

"Why would you think such a thing?"

"Well," I began, trying to speak a little bit slower this time. "I saw this man at the airport. He was looking at me, and he didn't leave with anyone. Now he is here in the same small town I am and he was staring at me again. But then something happened."

Thomas just kept staring at me, not saying a word. It was almost as if he was studying me, I thought.

"Some men came along in a car and pushed him into the backseat and sped off," I explained, trying not to sound deranged.

Again, Thomas just stood there staring at me.

"Did you hear what I said?" I asked, stepping back a pace.

"Yes. I heard what you said. Are you sure you are not confused? Perhaps he lives here. Perhaps he is visiting someone. There are over 50 million people living in England. This may all just be a coincidence. Maybe he was staring because he recognized you too and thought it was a bit ironic as well," Thomas rationalized.

"Okay, why did those men push him into the backseat of their car?" I demanded.

"Gambling debt?" he said with a grin, shrugging his shoulders.

And with that, I felt most of the wind leave my sails. My mind was racing again. Could it all be that simple and uncomplicated?

"You seem to have a flair for the dramatic," he said, then bridged the gap between us and kissed me on the lips.

I managed a slight laugh, but it was more out of nervousness than sincerity.

"Perhaps you are right," I said, but the whole time I was thinking I was not just going to let this go. I didn't know what was happening, but I was certainly going to find out. I looked at Thomas again and knew the conversation was over. He clearly thought I was either exaggerating the whole thing or I had not interpreted the situation correctly. Either way, he did not see the situation the way I did, and apparently there was nothing I could say to change his mind.

Thomas sat back down and continued to read his newspaper, and I decided to hop in the shower.

"I have arranged for a bit of sightseeing for us," Thomas said, looking up from his paper. "Perhaps you could do a bit of shopping as well, if you feel like it?"

"That sounds wonderful. I'll be out in a flash," I said, making my way to the bathroom and closing the door behind me.

I stood in the shower, my back to the nozzle, trying to relax my shoulder muscles. That was always where stress hit me first, right across the trapezius muscles. As the warm water began to work its magic, I thought perhaps a day out was exactly what I needed, a distraction to help clear my head. It would probably do me the world of good, I thought. And shopping? It was a gruelling task, but I knew I would take it like a trooper.

After I got out of the shower, brushed my hair and got dressed, I walked back into the other room to gather my purse. Arming myself with three credit cards, Thomas and I set out for the day. There was a multitude of clothing shops in Hythe, so we started there. Then, we purchased a day pass for the double-decker bus, number 711, that ventured into Folkestone, Lydd, Romney Marsh and Rye. All the towns were lovely, but Rye took my breath away. It was a picturesque little cinque-port town preserved magnificently to display its abounding history and culture. A sign on the town's Ypres Tower said it pre-dated the Norman Conquest. I loved anything to do with history, prehistory and culture and Thomas knew it. He knew exactly what I would love to see and planned our trip accordingly.

It was mid-afternoon when I finally noticed my stomach growling, so I suggested to Thomas that we find somewhere to settle for a bite to eat. We found a quaint little Tudor home that was converted into a café just off High Street. It seemed every High Street in England was the equivalent to every

Main Street in Ontario. It was the primary street that ran straight through the centre of each town.

We made our way through the café and onto the back patio where we sat underneath a marquee. A slight breeze was blowing and the sun was shining brightly in the sky.

I thought England was supposed to rain eternal.

I lifted my face towards the sun and closed my eyes. It was rejuvenating. The waitress came over, dressed in a black frilly dress and white apron. She also wore a white frilly cap on her head that reminded me of my Raggedy Ann doll I had growing up. We ordered bangers and mash, raisin scones and Sussex cream tea. There was now no doubt in my mind that I was going to go home ten pounds heavier than when I had arrived, but as I delved into my lunch, I knew it was a sacrifice I was willing to make.

After lunch, we continued on our journey and ventured into a number of antique shops. It was amazing what you could find in one. I bought a lovely King George V commemorative coin set from 1911, the year my grandmother was born, and Thomas bought a stunning ladies' cocktail watch and placed it on my wrist before we left the store.

"Thank you, Thomas. It's gorgeous," I said, looking down at it.

He smiled at me. "Come. There are more places I want to show you."

Thomas and I spent the rest of the day sightseeing, shopping, eating, drinking and most importantly, laughing. I could not remember the last time I laughed that much. It must have been after 10:00 p.m. by the time we finally straggled back to the inn.

CHAPTER 15

The next morning, I woke up feeling very tired. When my head hit the pillow last night, I was out like a light, but I only slept well for the first half of the night. The latter half of the night didn't go as well. I tossed and turned in between fitful fragments of sleep and bizarre dreams.

I lay in bed with my eyes wide open. I rolled over and tucked the king size navy blue duvet under my chin and looked towards the window. The sun was peaking through the shades and the floral-print curtains were gently swaying back and forth with the breeze that was making its way in through the crack in the window. Looked like another beautiful day in Southeast Kent, but I wasn't in the mood to enjoy it. It could have been my uneasy sleep that put me off; but, I think it had more to do with the fact that yesterday, and the day before that come to think of it, had been such an emotional roller coaster for me. I knew it was all starting to take its toll. I also knew I wasn't going to enjoy a lie in, so I tossed back the covers, swung my legs over the side of the bed and stretched. When I stood up, I winced.

"Ouch!"

Thomas rolled over and asked what was wrong.

"My feet are killing me," I said.

He laughed, and rolled back over.

"It was self inflicted," he said.

"A nicer man wouldn't have said that," I said, smacking him as I made my way over to the table where my laptop was.

As my laptop sprang to life and performed its melodious start up jingle, Thomas rolled back towards me and asked me what I was doing.

"Just checking my e-mail," I said.

"Frankie, you are on holiday now. Can it not wait? Come back to bed and I shall distract you," he said, smirking.

"Later," I said half-heartedly, but not before contemplating Thomas's offer rather descriptively in my head. "I still have responsibilities to attend to."

"Fine. But later you are mine," he said, as he pulled back the covers and walked into the bathroom naked. My god, he had an amazing body. It was fit, tanned, and muscular. Not at all like any surgeon I had ever imagined. Most, I thought, were probably pale and pallid from too many twenty-eight-hour days underneath the fluorescents.

I logged on to my e-mail account and the screen popped up requesting my password. I heard Thomas turn on the taps. I thought about him underneath the mist of the shower with drops of water gathering and glistening all over his body. I had to admit, even with his change in attributes, he was still truly spectacular to look at.

My laptop beeped, jarring my mind back to the task at hand and away from the thought of Thomas naked in the next room. I had thirteen e-mails, ten were business, two looked like spam, and the last one was from an unknown recipient. It was marked, 'Urgent.' Fearing an online virus, I automatically deleted it. Then for some reason unbeknownst to me, my curiosity got the better of me. I retrieved it from the trash folder, noticed there were no attachments, the first sign of a Trojan virus, and opened it. The e-mail contained nothing more than a hyperlink to another site. Strange, I thought. I clicked on the link and what I saw knocked me for six. It was a link to a London newspaper. The story headline read: Interpol Officer Found Dead: Police Suspect Murder. And there, beside the headline, was a photo of the blonde man I saw at Gatwick airport, the one who was chucked into the back of that sedan yesterday. I increased the size of the page and read on.

The body of a French Interpol officer was discovered this morning just outside of Holland Park. He was identified as Officer André Bruyere, 35, of Bourgogne, France. The details as to whether Officer Bruyere was vacationing or working in London have yet to be determined. Police spokespersons at the local level, and at MI5, are not commenting at this time stating a need for further investigation, although other police sources say they suspect foul play.

I heard Thomas shut off the shower, so I quickly closed my e-mail. How did men shower so quickly?

Again, my head was spinning. I quickly dismissed the idea of engaging Thomas in yet another conversation about any of this. I needed time to think.

A moment later, Thomas walked back into the room wearing the same variety of white towel I had originally met him in. Again, it was wrapped snugly around his middle, skilfully drawing attention to his six-pack amongst other areas of interest.

"Anything interesting?" he asked.

For some reason, his question caught me off guard. I don't know whether it was the way he looked at me, or the way he said it, but it was as if he knew. I looked at him for a moment before I said, "Just the usual."

He stood there and stared at me for several moments before he dropped his towel and began to get dressed. Why did I feel like he could see right through me? Perhaps it was just the look on my face that perplexed him.

"Would you like something to eat?" he asked, as he fastened the hook on his trousers and straightened the waist.

"Yes, I would. Would you be so kind as to bring something back for us?"

"Do you not wish to come with me? It looks quite nice out."

"Actually, I was planning on going for a run, but I don't quite feel up to it. I think I'll just have a nice long hot bath instead."

Thomas sauntered over to me, kissed me on the lips and said, "Of course."

Then he made his way to the front door, slipped on his shoes and turned to wink at me before he left.

I listened for him to descend the staircase all the way to the bottom before I reopened my e-mail. I must have re-read the newspaper article a dozen times before I shut down my laptop and dialled Marianne's number in Oakville. On the third ring, her answering machine clicked in, so I had no recourse but to leave her a quick message asking her to call me back as soon as possible. After I recited the phone number of the inn, I hung up praying she would call me back before Thomas returned.

Then, I snuggled up in one of the winged-back chairs and stared out the window watching a very industrious little grey-and-white-striped spider try to spin his web in the wind.

"What an uncomplicated life you lead, my little friend," I said aloud. "For you, it's all just a storm in a teacup isn't it?"

Then my thoughts ventured to my blonde acquaintance. What happened to you? Were you watching *me*? I was starting to feel a bit unnerved, so I got up and stretched my legs while I waited for Marianne to call back.

"Dinna fash yersel', Frankie," I heard in my head. It was a Scottish expression my grandmother used to say to me all the time. It meant not to worry yourself or something to that effect. I tried to think of what my grandmother would say to me at a time like this. It was sure to be something very practical that would put everything in perspective. God, I missed her.

The phone rang, and I ran to get it. It was Marianne, of course. As I said hello, I pulled the phone cord out from underneath the corner of the carpet, lifted it over the bureau, and tugged at it until I got enough slack to bring the whole unit over to the chair so I could sit down comfortably with it.

"Frankie?"

"Hey, stranger," I said, sitting down and trying to sound calmer than I was feeling.

"Sorry I missed your call, but you woke me out of a dead sleep."

"Damn, Marianne, forgive me, I forgot all about the five-hour time difference," I said, shaking my head.

"Never mind that, I'm up now. So? Where the hell are you? I can't believe you went to meet this guy without even telling me. Oh, that's right you did tell me. In an e-mail if I remember correctly," she said sarcastically.

"Marianne, please. I think I have a bit of a problem."

"Frankie, what is going on? Are you okay?"

"Yes and no," I said. "Oh, Marianne, I'm so bloody confused right now, I don't know what to think."

"Just tell me what the hell is going on, Frankie. You're scaring me."

I explained everything to her as she remained silent on the other end of the receiver. I told her about Thomas not meeting me at the airport; about the blonde man who was also at the airport but was now dead; about Thomas evading all my questions and basically telling me I was over-reacting to seeing the blonde man being kidnapped, and now about the anonymous e-mail with the link to the newspaper clipping.

"I don't know what the hell is going on, Frankie," Marianne said. "But I want you to come home. I don't like any of this. Where is Thomas now? What did he say about the murder?"

I couldn't keep up with her. "Marianne, please calm down. I need a clear head to think this through with me, okay? And, no, I haven't mentioned the newspaper clipping."

"Why not?" Marianne asked, lowering her voice.

"Because this could still just be a big misunderstanding."

"Is that what you think, Frankie? Really?"

"No, I don't," I said gravely. "But I'm not coming home yet either. I need to know what this is all about and what it has to do with me. Surely you can understand that?"

"Yes, I do, but I'm not just going to sit back and wait. Look, at least send me a copy of the newspaper clipping and let me mull it over, okay?"

"That would be wonderful. Thank you."

"Oh, and Frankie?"

"Yes?"

"Send me an e-mail with everything you know about Thomas as well."

"Why?" I asked, knowing full well why Marianne wanted it.

"Because we need to look at the whole picture, hon, we both know this."

"You're right, but what do I do in the meantime?"

"Be damn careful, that's what you should do, and take precautions. Always be on guard. Do you hear me? Keep your cell phone charged and never venture anywhere you can't get a hold of me."

"I promise."

"I'm sorry, Frankie, I don't mean to scare you any more than I'm sure you already are; but, I would much rather you be safe than sorry."

"I know," I said. "Please try not to worry."

I heard the front door close and someone making their way up the creaky stairs.

"I think Thomas is back. I have to go."

"Call me as soon as you can," Marianne said firmly.

"I will. Thanks, Mare. I don't know what I'd do without you."

I quickly hung up as I heard a key being put into the lock. Thomas made his way inside, his arms full of take-away cartons.

"I thought you were going to take a bath?" Thomas asked as he walked into the room and began placing the cartons on the table beside the winged-back chairs. I also saw him look directly at my laptop.

"I was, but I got distracted," I said. "What's on the menu?"

"Distracted with what?" Thomas asked, diverting his eyes away from me.

"Nothing really," I feigned. "Are you going to feed me or what?"

After two blatant attempts at deflecting the conversation, Thomas finally took the hint and let it go.

"I have a surprise for you. Close your eyes and hold out your hands."

I closed my eyes and felt Thomas place some thin cardboard paper in my hands.

"Open them," he said, as he grinned from ear to ear.

"Thomas!" I shrieked. "When did you get these?"

"Just before you arrived," he beamed. "How could I let you come all the way to England and not take you to a Premiership game?"

"Brilliant! When is it?" I asked, looking down at the tickets and turning them around to read them.

"This afternoon," he said. "Chelsea and Manchester United."

"So let me get this straight. Not only do I get to see an actual Premiership game, but I also get to see Cristiano Ronaldo as well? Not bad, Thomas," I said, laughing.

"I am sorry it is not Arsenal playing."

"Are you kidding me? This is fantastic. I am very grateful Thomas, thank you."

When it came to English football, the Gunners were my favourite team, bar none, but I also had my list of favourite players as well, and Cristiano was definitely at the top of the heap. When I watched him on the pitch, the whole world stood still and I stopped breathing. With Chelsea and Manchester United playing, it wasn't going to be hard to lose myself in all the excitement. It would definitely be the ultimate means of distraction for me. I absolutely lived for football, and Thomas knew it.

"You're the best," I beamed.

"I will take it out in trade later," Thomas said, laughing.

CHAPTER 16

After a leisurely breakfast, a discreet phone call to Marianne to say I'd call her tonight and a nice long run along the beachfront, I made my way back to the inn and began to get ready for the game. The drive to Chelsea was an hour and a half from Hythe, and I didn't want to be late. I couldn't believe I was going to see a Premiership game in person. I honestly believed it was the only sport that truly evoked unprecedented passion from both the players and the fans. With every game I watched, I felt the emotions of every person there, on and off the pitch. The players were veritable artists, and I was the fundamental aficionado.

On the way to the stadium, Thomas and I engaged in yet another one of our brilliant and stimulating conversations. I took it as the perfect opportunity to gently prod him for information, without sounding interrogative, and without making him suspicious of my motives. I tried to softly steer the conversation on to family, hoping he would open up and fill me in on a few things – information I could share with Marianne later. He willingly obliged.

I found out that while he was born in England, he only lived here for the first ten years of his life. By the time he was eleven, his parents moved to Germany. Later he went to high school in France and on to university in Switzerland. This, I concluded, was the reason for his unidentifiable accent. It was an amalgamation of several – all beautifully blended and distinctively unique to Thomas. Additionally, he said the reason he missed me in Gatwick was that the agency he worked for changed his itinerary without informing him. He ended up flying in the day before and couldn't contact me because he didn't have access to his e-mail. He also said he had a mate who lived in Folkestone whom he hadn't seen in several months. He knew he would eventually venture out that way to see him anyway, so he thought he'd get the visit out of the way so he and I could spend the duration of time we had together uninterrupted. He apologized for the misunderstanding, and he teased me for thinking it was all so cloak-and-dagger.

As for his change in appearance, I started to think it was perhaps just a new style that took his fancy. It was hard not to notice Thomas's distinctive taste in couture. He had quite a bit of well-tailored apparel strewn about our room. I naturally concluded his newly tinted hair and contact lenses were just part and parcel of his overall sense of corresponding fashion – ergo when he changed one, he probably changed them all. It was called a prerogative, I rationalized.

I never broached the subject of the two blurry photos or the different pitch in his voice because at this point I didn't want him to know about any of my additional trepidations. I wanted him to think I was over all my fundamental qualms and that I was just trying to enjoy our time together.

I never mentioned the Frenchman who was murdered either. I wanted to wait until I spoke with Marianne before I pursued that angle any further. All I wanted to do at this particular time was to enjoy the fresh air and to see my first in-person Premiership game.

I wondered if the fans would boo me if I threw myself onto the pitch and begged Cristiano Ronaldo to have his children.

Perhaps Thomas was not quite ready for that side of me yet.

CHAPTER 17

Stamford Bridge was crowded, as I had anticipated. The parking lot was congested, but the mood was invigorating and infectious. I smiled. I could actually feel the collective heartbeats of forty-two-thousand elated fans.

It was just slightly cooler today, but I figured while I didn't appreciate the drop in the temperature, I knew the players would. Thomas and I finally found a parking spot and began to make our way towards the front gates. We had remarkable seats. We were on the West Lower Tier, almost dead centre. I sat down while Thomas went to get us some essential provisions, like chips, or crisps as they were called in Britain, and sodas. He returned with a barrage of edibles and a game shirt for me.

"Thank you, Thomas," I said, laughing.

We settled in and waited for the players to take the pitch. As they all walked onto the field, my heart began to race. Chelsea and Manchester United were only three points away from each other in the standings, so the pressure you could feel in the stadium was rather substantial. Thomas looked over at me and smiled. I guess the look on my face said it all.

It was an exhilarating match. By half-time, the Blues had possession of the ball forty-seven per cent of the time and the Red Devils had it fifty-three per cent. The score was tied at 1-1. I was surprised Thomas had any ear drums left from me screaming in them the majority of the time. It took me no time at all to learn some of the local football chants. In fact, after some of the local spectators heard my Canadian accent, they took it upon themselves to personally teach me the words knowing I was a tourist. My favourite was entitled, *Twelve Men*. It was meant to insult a bias referee who seemed to be favouring one team over the other. The whole experience was absolutely amazing. I refused to sing anything against Manchester United though.

As the whistle blew signalling half-time, Thomas said he wanted to take another look around the concession stands. I needed the bathroom, so I said I would go with him. As Thomas made his way towards the vendors, I made my way to the ladies' room very excited and eagerly awaiting the start of the second half of the match.

When I was done, I walked out of the washroom and looked up and down the long corridor for Thomas. I thought I spotted him at the far north end of the building speaking with two men by a set of fire doors. I squinted to make sure it was him and began to make my way towards them. All of a sudden, I saw one of the men hit Thomas square across the jaw and again in the stomach. I immediately started running towards them, but the men managed to push Thomas out of the emergency doors before I could get to them. As I got to the doors, I started shaking them violently, trying to open them but something was wedged up against them on the other side and I couldn't budge them. I continued banging on the doors yelling Thomas's name, but to no avail. I turned frantically trying to find a security person, but I was at the long end of the hallway and didn't know where to begin to look. The only people within calling distance were already making their way back to their seats for the second half of the game. No one seemed to notice what happened.

I turned and ran out the nearest exit doors I could find and into the parking lot hysterically searching for any sign of Thomas. I couldn't see him anywhere. I heard a set of screeching tires behind me and whipped my head around to see a dark grey sedan speeding out of the parking lot heading up Fulham Road towards Earls Court Station.

"Thomas!" I screamed, as I watched his handsome face looking back at me from the backseat of the car.

I immediately felt my heart sink. I placed my hands over my face and began to sob as the realization hit me. It was the same sedan I saw in Hythe, and those men were probably the same men who abducted the Frenchman, and in all likelihood, murdered him.

CHAPTER 18

With trembling legs, I made my way back into the stadium through the front doors and found the security desk. I began to explain what happened to a tall, slender, security officer with a shock of auburn hair. He was standing alongside a rather young-looking man with brown hair and a modicum of freckles across his nose. Two minutes into the conversation, I quickly realized I wasn't making much sense and probably sounded like I was becoming a bit unhinged. They listened intently for another few minutes and then began to look back and forth at each other, probably surmising I was insane as far as they were concerned. I mean, what could I truly tell them anyway? I only knew what Thomas had told me, and apparently I now had to question how much of that information was actually true. Thomas obviously left out a few fundamental details about his life, something that was blatantly obvious to me now. I began to mentally berate myself, then paused thinking of what to say next. The younger man said he would contact the local authorities for me, if indeed I wanted to explain it all to them too.

Ostensibly, they were not quite sure what to make out of the whole situation, and regrettably, neither did I. I told them not to bother and that it was probably a big misunderstanding, which seemed to be much easier for them to believe than the reality of it all.

I left the security desk quietly and headed out to the parking lot. Thank god Thomas asked me to hang on to the keys for the rental car. I'm not sure I would know how to hot wire a car.

After I found the car, I drove very unsure of myself past Earls Court, above the Hammersmith flyover, onto the A4 and finally onto the M25 to head back towards Hythe.

Nothing says panic like having to drive on the opposite side of the road for the first time in my life while trying to get my head wrapped around the fact that the man with whom I have been sleeping with was just kidnapped in broad daylight right in front of my eyes.

I think half a dozen people flipped me the bird on the thoroughfare on my way back to the inn. I couldn't blame them really. I wasn't doing much in the way of dispelling the bad-woman-driver myth. I felt very lucky to have made it back in one piece, or not to have taken out several other people along the way. I parked the car outside the inn and took the stairs up to our room by twos. I desperately needed to talk to Marianne.

As I entered our room, I paused in mid-step. Something felt strange to me. I felt as if someone had been in our room, someone other than housekeeping. I couldn't quite put my finger on it. Damn these feelings of mine, I thought. Nothing seemed to be missing or out of place; yet, I felt as if the room had been violated somehow. Shaking my head as if I could literally shake the unpleasant feeling from my senses, I sat down in one of the winged-back chairs, wiped the sweat from my brow and dialled Marianne's number. She answered on the first ring.

"Frankie?" she said anxiously, even before saying hello.

"Marianne, you are never going to believe what just happened," I stammered, not doing a very good job at keeping my composure.

"Thomas was kidnapped!" I said.

"What?" Marianne yelled into the receiver.

"We were at a football match in Chelsea. I went to the ladies' room, and when I came out two men were talking to Thomas. Then one of them hit him, pushed him out the emergency exit doors and into a car. And guess what?" I said breathlessly. "It was the same car that took that French Interpol officer!"

"Did you go to the police?" Marianne asked, sounding even more distraught. "I tried to explain it to two security guards but ended up feeling like an idiot. They looked at me like I was crackers! So I drove straight back here and called you instead. Marianne, what the hell am I going to do?"

"Honey, I'm afraid it gets worse," Marianne said, clearing her throat.

I paused fearing the worst.

"I take it you've found something then?" I asked, scarcely recognizing my own voice. Actually, it's what I didn't find that disconcerts me, Frankie. There is no Thomas Bissett working for the International Association of Volunteer Physicians. In fact, I had a friend run a search through the UK database of surgeons, and there is no Thomas Bissett registered who even remotely matches the criteria of Thomas."

"Are you sure? I asked, now pacing back and forth in front of my chair. There must be dozens of surgeons named Thomas Bissett in the UK."

"Yes, but they are either the wrong ethnicity or age, or they specialize in something totally different. Frankie, this came from a very reputable private investigative firm. Trust me," she said, and then paused for a second. "Hang on, there's more. I sifted through several online newspapers from France and found a profile piece on that Interpol agent who was murdered. It seems our Mr. Bruyere was a specialized agent who had been under internal investigation for some time. Guess what he specialized in?"

"What?" I said, nervously rubbing my temple.

"Foreign espionage."

"So who the hell was he tracking?" I barked.

"I have no idea, Frankie, but somehow Thomas is caught up in all of this. I am worried about you. You have to go to the police."

"And say what, Mare? That I met a guy over the Internet flew to another country to meet him and watched him get kidnapped at a football game? Can you imagine the questions? What's his name, Miss? Gee, I'm not sure, officer. Do you know where he lives, Miss? Gee, I'm not sure of that either, officer. I'd be the laughing stock of the whole of England's law enforcement team."

"Okay, calm down," she said. "I see your point. You can always come home you know."

"No way. I want to know what the hell happened. It's better if I stay and figure it out from here."

"That's just crazy, Frankie. Please come home."

"I'm sorry, Mare. I'll call you as soon as I can."

As I hung up the receiver, I walked over to the front window and wrapped my arms around myself. I felt the warm sting of tears begin to well up behind my eyelids. I stood there as they began to spill down my face and drip onto my arms, carrying with them all my despondency. It was a release I desperately needed.

CHAPTER 19

In all actuality only twenty minutes had passed, but it seemed like hours before I was finally able to compose myself. I knew I couldn't fall apart anymore. I wasn't used to losing control of my emotions like that. Then again, I wasn't used to feeling so lost and frightened either. I tried to shake it off and turned towards the bathroom with the intention of splashing cold water on my face when I walked dead into Thomas's suitcase.

"Well, well, well," I said aloud, quickly starting to gain back my lost senses.

As I lifted the oversized case onto the bed, I began to pray it wouldn't be locked. With two swift clicks, they both swung open.

"Thank you, Thomas."

Most of Thomas's things were already in the side bureau or hung up in the wardrobe, so all I found inside his suitcase were some extra toiletries and a few spare items of clothing. As I began to check the lining pockets, I suddenly thought about his carry-on that was tucked inside the little cubby beside the hall table.

I walked over to the cubby and gently wedged the black leather bag out of its holding spot. Unfortunately, this one was locked, but I only had to fiddle with it for a few minutes before I was able to budge it. With one half sheer determination, and one half handy nail file, I was able to wedge the lock open. Suitcase locks aren't exactly made with top-of-the-line security.

I started riffling through it, but most of the content seemed inconsequential to me. There were some price tags that were torn from some clothing he must have purchased, there were some brochures of places to visit, probably with me in mind;

but, then I came across something I didn't expect. Wrapped up very carefully with a dirty brown elastic band, I found four passports.

My heart sank.

As I removed the elastic band with shaky hands, my worst fears were confirmed. There was one for Tomás Alvarez, place of birth Mexico; there was another one for Thomas Bissett, place of birth England; there was another one for Tommaso Rossi, place of birth Italy; and the last one was for Thomas Grimstad, place of birth Sweden.

At this point, I was veritably livid. I scrutinized over each and every scrap of paper I picked up, no matter how insignificant they originally seemed. My ego was now taking a backseat to my journalistic instincts.

"Okay, Frankie," I said aloud. "It is time to take your personal attachment out of the equation."

My sheer determination for the truth was now surfacing stronger than ever. I continued to search through the bag and came across a credit card bill with one of Thomas's pseudonyms on it. The address was in Karlskoga, Sweden. It only took me fifteen minutes and I was booked on the next flight out, which happened to be at 7:30 a.m. the following morning.

I love modern technology.

I sat down in one of the winged-back chairs and gently rubbed my thumb over one of Thomas's passport photos.

"Why all the lies, Thomas?" I asked, staring down at it.

I got up from the chair and found a pen and a piece of paper. I began to jot down everything I knew and everything that had happened. I added as much detail as I could and began to draw arrows between events and timelines trying to make as many logical connections as I could.

It was a habitual exercise I formed early on in my journalism career. I studied the paper for a while and began to add hypotheses to it. Being a left-brain thinker, I knew the diagrams would help me make sense of the situation, if it was indeed possible to extract logic out of this one.

An hour later, my stomach growled and jarred me back to reality. I needed a break from writing anyway, so I put my notes down on the table and headed downstairs to order something to eat, clutching Thomas's carry-on bag in my hand. Hopefully, there would be no one in the sitting room so I could quietly go through it again while I was eating.

Mrs. Simpson was magnificently accommodating, as usual, and offered me a private sitting room to enjoy my tea and scones with clotted cream and fresh quince jam. No point in suffering anymore than I had to.

I emptied the contents of Thomas's bag onto the table and found nothing more than I did in the room. Feeling a bit defeated, I sat back to sip my tea. I couldn't help but fixate on how good Thomas had been at deceit, or at least how hard he tried to be. When I truly thought about it, though, he hadn't really hidden things that well, at least not if I gave myself credit and actually considered how many times red flags went off in my head. I mentally pored over everything that had transpired and concluded I should have trusted, and ultimately followed, my original gut instincts. I thought about all the events leading up to this and all the times I had questioned things. I knew deep down inside things were amiss, but I still continued to make excuses and rationalize his actions. He even pretended to be a damn doctor, I thought. Actually, he pretended to be a doctor in war-torn Lebanon. He knew I'd be taken in by that fact. Was he ever really there? I wondered.

I began to go over our conversations in as much detail as I could. I wondered if I had told him what I did for a living before he told me about Lebanon. I couldn't remember now. I was trying desperately to make even more connections. Why me at all? Was it purely coincidental? Yes, it must have been, I rationalized. I was the one who contacted him, not vice versa. My mind was totally taken over by unanswered questions. I sat there, staring at Thomas's bag, trying to put things in perspective, when all of a sudden it hit me. Without hesitation, I picked up the bag and started to check the inner lining of it, and then, I felt it.

It was a heavy paper, just inside the lining of the bag. I used my butter knife, while looking around for Mrs. Simpson fearing she'd think I was losing my marbles, and gently tore open the stitching. I slid my hand inside and produced a five-by-seven photo. When I turned it around to see who it was, I thought I was going to be sick. It was a photo of the French Interpol agent that was murdered and Józef – my father.

CHAPTER 20

The room was spinning faster than I could stand it. I got up from the table, clutching everything in my arms protectively, ran up the stairs as fast as I could, practically broke the key off in the lock, bolted into the bathroom, leaned over the toilet and threw up.

How could this be happening to me? Not Józef. Not now. Not again. I desperately needed to talk to someone. I suddenly felt so alone. I couldn't even call Marianne about this. I could never explain it to her. I could never explain it to anyone.

Mentally exhausted and physically ill, I curled up at the end of the bed and tried to get my head wrapped around what had just transpired. It wasn't a coincidence after all. Thomas sought me out on purpose. But why? And, more importantly, how was Józef connected to it?

I lay on the bed for almost an hour staring at the ceiling and feeling totally exhausted. I could not believe what was happening.

"How the hell did you end up in this mess, Francesca?"

I tried to go over each and every scenario, but it was all in vain. I felt like my brain was completely shutting down. I finally closed my eyes and tried to steady my thoughts.

It was dark out now and as I lay there, I heard the key being inserted into the lock. I couldn't see anything. It was too black. I heard the door open. I still couldn't see. Suddenly a hand clamped itself over my mouth as I struggled to catch my breath. The lamp beside the bed went on and Thomas stood overtop of me, his eyes begging me not to scream. I must have looked horrified. He let go of my mouth.

"Thomas, what is going on? Who are you? What do you want with me?" I stammered.

"Quickly, we must leave now. They are going to kill us both," he said, in a forced whisper.

"But...," I stammered.

"Now, Frankie! We must go now."

I heard someone else coming up the creaky stairs. I started to panic and instantly broke out in a sweat. I rolled over and heard myself yell, NO!!!

That must have been what woke me. I must have called out in my sleep. It was hard to focus. I heard Mrs. Simpson in the hallway outside my door.

"Are you all right, pet?" she asked.

"Yes, Mrs. Simpson. I just had a bad dream. I'm all right now. Thank you."

"Okay, dear, if you're sure. If you need anything, you know where to find me."

"Thank you," I said, still unsure of my surroundings.

I heard her begin to hum to herself again as she went about her business. I sat up and looked at the clock at the edge of the nightstand. It was only 10:22 p.m.

CHAPTER 21

My lurid dream rattled me a bit so I wasn't too keen on the idea of falling back asleep. Instead, I sat up, plumped up my pillows, tucked them behind me and leaned back against the headboard. I reached over to turn on the nightlight on Thomas's side of the bed and caught a fleeting whiff of his cologne. It was an aroma I could have done without at the moment.

I leaned back toward my side of the bed and sighed. I just couldn't figure it out. My mind went over every possible scenario it could trying to figure out who Thomas was, what he wanted from me, how he found me, and more decisively, how he managed to get *me* to contact *him*.

Several details were quite clear. First, Thomas sought me out on purpose. Second, Józef was intricately involved, a detail that upset me deeply. Third, Thomas was not who he claimed to be. Fourth, all my initial suspicions were justified – a mistake I would not make a second time. There was one more absolute I was convinced of as well. I was probably going to have to confront my past, and in all likelihood, I was probably going to have to confront Józef – something I desperately wished to circumvent. There were other details, however, that were not so clear. Like, what did Thomas want from me and how was I going to get to the bottom of it all?

CHAPTER 22

I was born Francesca Maria Kowalski. I cringe when I think of that name. It sickens me. That name epitomizes shame, hatred, and resentment. I must force myself to say it aloud, and it brings tears to my eyes every time I have to think about it. It exemplifies a young girl so very angry at the world, and now it seems I must face the demons of my past that have haunted me for almost twenty years.

Bradford was my mother's maiden name. My father was, and most likely still is, part of the Polish mafia operating out of Warsaw. I spent the majority of my childhood under his oppressing rule and vicious tongue. He was always right, and I feared him at every turn. He drove my mother to alcoholism, which eventually killed her; and, he turned my older brother, Victor, into someone I did not respect. He is dead now too. The details of his death are still a mystery to me. I never wanted to know.

One day after school, I came home to find my grandmother waiting for me on the front porch. She told me my father, Józef, was gone and she was going to be caring for me from then on. I never knew what happened and never asked. I couldn't have been happier.

The last time I remember seeing Józef, the night before he left, I was in my room getting ready for bed. He called me out of my bedroom saying he wanted to show me something. As I approached the living room, I saw my little black cat, Samantha, on his lap. He was choking her and laughing. Her eyes were bugging out of her head and she was visibly scared. She struggled with asphyxiation as she looked straight at me. I wanted to run and save her, but I feared him too much. I knew the ramifications for challenging him and they were too grave to even consider. So, I watched. It was all I could do. I watched his face too. It gave him such pleasure every time he squeezed. Again and again.

I wanted him dead.

When my grandmother took me away, we settled in Ontario. From then on, I was only known as Francesca Bradford, and I never looked back. I never knew what happened to Józef. I never really cared.

CHAPTER 23

I slept intermittently throughout the night while still propped up on my pillows and with the nightlight still on. My eyes felt gritty as I finally dragged myself out of bed, but by 5:30 a.m., I was showered and packed. I called a taxi and made my way downstairs to wait for it. I was surprised to find Mrs. Simpson awake at that hour, but there she was as fresh as a daisy and as jovial as ever.

"Are you leaving us, Frankie?" she asked, walking towards me with a feather duster in her hand.

"Yes, I'm sorry, but I have to fly to Sweden on business. It's all very last minute, I'm afraid," I said, trying to sound light-hearted.

"And Mr. Bissett? Will he be going with you?"

"I'm afraid Thomas has his own agenda. I'm not sure what he'll be doing. I'm not even sure what to do with his things. Actually, Mrs. Simpson, I've left a few things of my own up there as well. I'm afraid I can only manage one bag on this trip. Would you mind helping me out with that? I'll leave some money for you, of course."

"Don't you worry about a thing, my pet. I'll tuck them away for now. We have plenty of space," she said.

She looked at me a bit longer. It was as if she knew how I was feeling. It must have shown on my face. No matter how hard I tried to hide my emotions, my face always defied me.

"Are you all right, love?" she asked, walking even closer to me now.

"I feel like such a fool," I said, as a single tear made its way down my cheek. I couldn't help it. It wasn't like me to confide in strangers, and it certainly wasn't like me to cry in front of one, but I felt so alone. She had such a warmth about her I just couldn't help myself. She handed me the tissue she had tucked into the cuff of her sleeve and patted my shoulder. "Affairs of the heart are never as simple as we'd like them to be," she offered. "Things may just work out for the two of you yet."

I quickly wiped away the wet streak on my cheek just as it began to sting. I gave her a brief hug, thanked her for all her lovely hospitality, then walked out the front door and into the waiting taxi. She waved to me as the cab pulled away, its tires crunching down on the gravel driveway. She made me miss my grandmother even more.

CHAPTER 24

The flight to Sweden went by fairly quickly. Gatwick to Stockholm Arlanda airport was only five hours, but then I was going to have to take a bus an additional two hundred kilometres to Karlskoga. This was the quickest route I could find on such short notice. I didn't mind. I knew it would give me some extra time to calm myself before I got to Karlskoga

After the plane landed, I made my way through baggage claim and customs in record time. Even though Arlanda was a relatively small airport, compared to most I had been in, it was still very organized and laid out in such a way that people moved through it very quickly. It was set up in a very efficient manner that seemed to almost eliminate passenger congestion. The Swedes really know how to do things right, I thought. I was reading a magazine article on the plane that said Sweden was taking the initiative to completely wean itself off oil by the year 2020. The country of nine million was going to be the world's first oil-free country. Bravo, I thought. I hope more follow suit.

The *flygbussar*, or *airport coaches*, were parked just across from the airport. I looked over and noticed several waiting in their designated bays. I scurried out of the airport and made my way across the street to see if I could find the one heading to Karlskoga. I was in luck. It was a rather large blue and white luxury coach, parked in the second slot from the end.

After the driver punched a hole in my ticket, I made my way towards the back of the coach, slung my carry-on bag into the overhead luggage rack and sat down in the seat closest to the window. I wanted a seat near the back for a bit more privacy. The coach was relatively empty and most passengers were sitting directly behind the driver, so it was easy to segregate myself.

I kicked off my shoes, tucked them under the seat in front of me and called Marianne on my mobile phone. My feet were killing me. I lifted up my left foot and gave it a bit of a massage as I balanced my phone between my ear and shoulder, which wasn't easy to do with a thin mobile phone. After five rings, Marianne's voice mail kicked in. All I could do was leave a message. I reclined my seat and tried to think of my next logical move as the bus pulled out. I couldn't come up with one; I was just going to have to wing it.

A few minutes later, my phone rang. I didn't have to check the call display. I knew it was Marianne.

"Hey, Mare. Thanks for getting back to me so quickly," I said.

"Frankie?" It was a male voice.

I almost gave myself whiplash as I bolted upright in my seat.

"Thomas?" I yelled into the phone. There was no answer. The line was dead.

"Nooo!" I yelled, trying desperately to get the line back, but I knew it was hopeless. I looked down at my phone. It read, 'No service.'

I felt like throwing the bloody phone out the window. My heart was racing, and I was totally incensed at this point, but as I looked around, I knew I was going to have to quickly calm myself down. People were starting to turn around and stare.

Damn. Was that really Thomas on the other end of the phone? It was too hard to tell, but it was definitely a man's voice. All I could do was sit and pray that whoever it was would call me back. I sat there staring at my phone, refusing to even blink. I stared directly at the signal bars, imploring them to stay at full strength. Ten minutes later, it rang again. I answered it in less than half a ring.

"Hello?" I said anxiously.

"It's me. Have you heard anything yet?" It was Marianne. I exhaled slowly and gradually dropped my shoulders as I reclined back in my seat again.

"Yes, and no," I said, not sure how to explain things to her without actually having to explain Józef as well.

"I'm on my way to Sweden."

"Sweden! Why on earth are you going to Sweden?"

"I found a credit card statement in Thomas's suitcase. It had a Swedish address on it. I'm following it up as a lead."

"Frankie, I don't think this is something you should be pursuing," she said, sounding very serious. "This is not an assignment. You have no protection there."

"Too late," I said. "I've already landed and I'm on my way to Thomas's apartment. Please, Mare, I need you to support me on this."

There was a brief pause.

"Are you still there?" I asked.

"I'm here," she said, sighing. "So, I'm assuming you haven't heard anything yet?"

She knew she couldn't change my mind.

"I just got a phone call from someone, a man, but the connection was dropped, so I really couldn't say one way or another whether it was Thomas."

"Did it sound like him?" she asked.

"It was too quick to tell," I said.

Marianne could sense my total aggravation over this whole thing. Doing her best to support me, she said, "I'm sure you will find some answers soon."

There was really not too much she could say at this point anyway.

"Listen, I want you to take down this address, just in case we lose contact," I said to her.

"You'd better not lose contact with me," she said, then asked for the address.

"It's Strand Gatan 30, Karlskoga, Sweden."

"Got it. Is that all it says?"

"Yes. I should be there sometime late this afternoon."

"Frankie, not to rain on your parade, but what exactly do you expect to find there?"

"I wish I knew. My whole life just seems so upside down right now. I don't feel like I have control over anything anymore."

"You know, Frankie. There is an alternative," she said. "I could fly out and meet you."

"No way!" I said adamantly. "I want you exactly where you are, where I know you are safe. You mean way too much to me for me to drag you into this too. I'll be in touch as soon as I can. I promise."

"You are too wilful, did you know that?" Marianne said, sighing.

"You know me, Mare. I'd rather beg for forgiveness than ask for permission."

"Just remember you have options, Frankie."

But as we hung up, it became very clear to me that all my options were gone. Thomas had already seen to that.

CHAPTER 25

I took a taxi from the Karlskoga bus station to Thomas's apartment building and arrived just after 5:30 p.m. I had to adjust my watch again to make up for the loss of yet another hour. Eventually these shifts in time were going to catch up with me, I thought.

As I approached the main door, I wondered how I was going to get into the building, and Thomas's apartment, without any keys. I stepped inside the lobby and looked on the main board to search for his name. I found it within seconds, despite the Swedish abbreviations. It didn't take a rocket scientist to figure out that 1TR, 2TR and 3TR were floor levels. Although the board told me Thomas's apartment was on the third floor, it didn't tell me what apartment he was in, but I figured I would cross that bridge once I actually got inside the building. I pushed the buzzer for Thomas's apartment, just in case. There was no answer. I have no idea what I would have done had he answered it. I had no alternative but to wait for someone to either enter or exit the building and hope they would let me in.

Within minutes, an elderly couple came strolling up the walkway. The woman was carrying a miniature grey schnauzer in her arms dressed in some sort of green dog coat.

As they entered the building, the woman smiled at me. I smiled back and patted my pockets trying to indicate I had lost my keys. While I knew most Swedes spoke English, I still feared saying anything to her just in case she lapsed into Swedish. I did not want to draw any undue attention to myself. I already felt like an idiot trying to communicate with her through my bizarre rendition of charades.

Note to self. Learn a Scandinavian language.

She said something in Swedish and allowed me to follow them into the building. I couldn't even utter a thank you to her. All I could do was shrug and smile. She smiled back and said something to the gentleman she was with. Then he smiled at me in sort of a sympathetic way. I think they thought I was mute.

There were no apartment numbers on any of the doors in the building, but seeing as there were only three apartments per floor, Thomas's apartment was relatively easy to locate. It could also have been the fact his door had a name plate on it that read, *T. Grimstad.*

The lock on Thomas's door was not a deadbolt. It was a simple ball-shaped knob with a rounded latch. I looked up and mouthed the words, thank you. I was a firm believer in fate. These Swedes were really trusting, I thought. My door at home had two locks and a chain, and I lived in a nice neighbourhood.

With two straight jabs of my credit card, I was in.

"You should really do something about your lack of security, Thomas," I whispered to myself.

I gently pushed the door open and glanced inside. There was no noise coming from within, so I stepped into the apartment and flicked on the first light switch I found. The hallway was dim and empty. Feeling a bit braver, I called out this time, still dreading someone would answer me back. There was nothing but silence. I closed the door behind me and gradually inched my way forward, wiping some perspiration from my forehead. I was not used to breaking and entering. It was dreadfully nerve-wracking. I wondered how people could actually do it for a living.

I ventured forward and turned on another light. Straight ahead was the kitchen, to the left a bathroom with a stand-up shower, and to the right was the living room and a door I presumed led to some kind of balcony. All the rooms were colourless with a sparse amount of furniture in them.

As I scanned the room, I noticed something else that was odd. There were no photos. None. In fact, there was nothing in the whole apartment that personalized it at all. Obviously, just a place to sleep, I surmised.

Feeling much braver, I started going through some of the drawers in the living room, which apparently doubled as a bedroom. Most were empty, but one held some additional bills, all with Thomas's name on them, and all addressed to this apartment. Well, at least I knew I had the right apartment and I wasn't going to scare the hell out of some poor unsuspecting Swede.

I tossed the bills back into the drawer and sat down on the end of the futon to think. I needed outside eyes for this, I thought. I couldn't see the forest for the trees anymore. I picked up my mobile phone and tried to call Marianne, but her line was engaged. It was probably better not to speak with her right now anyway. The last thing I wanted to do was lie to her anymore than I already had. Omitting information still falls under the category of lying in my books no matter what kind of spin you put on it. It would be too hard to answer her questions without telling her the whole truth.

I got up to look out the window. There was a balcony out there. I stood there wondering who Thomas really was. Then I thought about the photo I found. I wondered what I would do if I had to come face to face with Józef. It had been a long time, but he still frightened the daylights out of me. I turned around to survey the room again. There had to be something here that would give me some answers, I thought. I walked over to the nightstand and began to rummage through its drawers as well.

Then, I heard a key go into the lock. My heart began to race and my hands instantly broke out in a sweat. I looked around for somewhere to hide, but immediately knew it was futile. I quickly remembered the balcony and ducked onto it hoping I could effectively hide there and still see who was entering the apartment. I stood just outside the balcony door and peered into the apartment through the crack between the trim and the curtain. I tried to steady my breathing. Was it Thomas? I wondered.

I stood as still as I could, not even daring to breathe. I watched carefully as two men entered the apartment. I did not recognize them. Then again, I didn't expect to. I overheard one of them say, "She must be here. The door wasn't locked. Check the balcony."

I froze. She must be here? Did they mean me? How the hell would they know I was here? How would they know who I was? I watched as the taller man started to make his way towards the balcony door as the other man entered the kitchen. I had to get away from them. I looked down. I had no choice. I had to scale down the balconies. As swiftly as I could, I swung my purse over my neck and shoulder and lifted my legs over the metal edge, gaining as much balance as I could before lowering myself onto the outside of the railing. I quickly wiped my clammy hands on my pants one by one, bent my knees and grabbed the lower railing. I let my legs fall hoping to locate the top of the next balcony. I did. From there, I let go of the bottom railing and clung on to the cement base until I gained my balance again. I looked down. It would be fairly easy to jump onto the next balcony as long as I could balance myself well. I was shaky, but was able to manoeuvre onto the second-floor balcony quite efficiently. I mentally thanked my grandmother for sending me to gymnastics and began the process all over again, trying to make it to the ground level before I was noticed. It was too late. Before I could make it to the next railing, I looked up and saw the face of the taller of the two men staring down at me.

"There," he yelled, pointing straight at me. "She's climbing down the balconies."

As quickly as I could, I manoeuvred myself to the bottom railing of the second floor balcony. From there, I was going to have to jump. Time was running out. They would be down those stairs in no time, I thought. I pushed myself out from the cement base and hoped for the best. It was not as far down as I had originally thought. I landed with a bit of a thud, but was very grateful I had landed on the grass and not the pavement.

I stood up just as the two men were exiting the building.

"There she is," one of them yelled.

I ran as fast as I could past several ground-level apartments, then around the corner of the building looking desperately for somewhere to hide. As I took the corner, I felt an immense thud and felt the air leave my lungs. I was stopped dead in my tracks. I had run straight into someone. The last thing I remember was feeling the sharp pain of being struck on the head. There must have been more than two of them. Then there was total blackness.

CHAPTER 26

As Frankie lay unconscious in the backseat, the burgundy Vauxhall Vectra was making its way through some drizzle and down the E18 at 90 kilometres an hour, ten kilometres under the speed limit displayed on the motorway's electronic signs – they did not want to attract any unwarranted attention. Beyonce's mesmeric vocals were erupting out of the radio. The two men in the front seat were staring straight ahead awaiting instructions. Then, a cell phone rang. The man in the passenger seat answered it. He knew who was calling.

A stern male voice said, "Did you complete the task?"

"Yes, she's here," he answered, looking behind him. "And, don't worry, she's still unconscious. She will have no idea where she is."

"Take her to the location we discussed and find out what the connection is."

"Yes, sir. What do we do with her when it's done?"

"Just complete the first task, then you will receive further instructions. Do not underestimate her, Agent Logan. She is not as innocuous as she seems."

"Yes sir."

"Where are agents Spencer and Philpott?"

"They left as soon as we had her."

"Carry on then."

Then there was silence and the connection was broken.

CHAPTER 27

I woke up on a large antique wooden chair with a splitting headache. My feet and hands were tied and my mouth was gagged. I could feel the caked blood on my face. As I lifted my head, the dried blood cracked and started to itch. My head was pounding so loudly, I could barely hear myself think. The room was badly lit and off in the distance I could hear the mutter of voices. Male voices. I looked around, feeling quite lethargic and nauseated. As my eyes began to focus, I realized I was in a cellar. At least it looked and smelled like a cellar. There was an old wrought iron wine rack, empty and wedged underneath the staircase directly in front of me. There was a work bench, directly to my right, that was covered with old paint cans and glass jars filled with nuts and bolts. Above the bench, there was a small window, caked with grime and laden with cobwebs. It was allowing some fragment of sunlight to penetrate the dimness of the room, but the tiny streaks of light did nothing more than illuminate the millions of dust particles floating through the air around me. Off to my left, there was a small room with a slanted yellow door that barely hung on one hinge. The door was closed, shy of about an inch or two, and there was a light coming from within it. As I tried to sit upright, the chair underneath me creaked. I heard a voice say, "I think she's coming to. Go check on her."

The door to the undersized room scraped against the floor as it opened. A rather stout man emerged, wearing a red toque, beige sweater, and grey penny loafers. I didn't have to look at the rest of his attire. There was already no accounting for taste. As he walked towards me, I sat up as high and straight as I could. It was a pride thing. I wanted to yell at him, but the gag in my mouth seemed to hinder that initiative. All I could do was wait to see what he would do.

"Pretty li'l thing aren't you?" he said in a Welsh accent.

I glared at him.

He glared back.

"Okay, let's get the hanky out of your mouth so we can chat, yeah?"

As he approached the chair, I watched him very carefully. He stood in front of me, almost straddling me, an obvious intimidation tactic, then reached around to the back of my head to untie the vile tasting piece of cloth in my mouth.

It was glued to the corners of my mouth by my own saliva and it ripped some skin away as he removed it, but I refused to call out in pain. He backed away, still staring at me. We stared at each other for several more moments.

Then I said, "I can see this is going to be one of those intellectual conversations. You know, I-N-T-E-L-L-E-C-T-U-A-L."

He smiled smugly, casually walked over to me and swiftly backhanded me across my jaw. My head jerked painfully to the side and back again.

"Let's try this again shall we?" he asked, not the least bit ruffled.

I said nothing.

"I'll get straight to the point. We want to know where Józef is."

Still, I said nothing.

He started walking towards me again, then bent down and lifted my face towards his. His face was now only centimetres from mine. His breath was acrid and reeked of stale cigarettes and bitter coffee.

"Cooperate and you can go home," he said. Then he squeezed my face hard and said, "Don't cooperate, and you and I are not going to get along very well. I'm not a patient person, so don't waste too much of my time here darlin'."

I looked into his eyes and said, "If you mean my father, I haven't seen that bastard in over twenty years. It's a tradition I plan on maintaining."

He stood back and surveyed my face, probably trying to determine if I was telling the truth or not. I continued to keep eye contact with him.

"Wait here," he said, laughing and tousling my hair. He walked back into the tiny room and began chatting with whoever was in there with him. A few moments later, he emerged. I looked down at his hand then back up to his face, then down at his hand again. He was grinning and holding a syringe.

CHAPTER 28

I began to struggle as he walked towards me, desperately trying to loosen the ropes that imprisoned me. All he did was laugh. He moved closer and stood towering overtop of me now, and I began to scream. He walked behind me, clamped his strong hand over my mouth and jerked my head to the side. His hands were calloused and smelled of motor oil. He bent down, his lips close to my ear and whispered, "Do that again, and I'll snap your pretty li'l neck. Do I make myself clear?"

I hesitated, and then nodded.

He let go and tried to lift the sleeve of my sweater, but it was in vain. I was thrashing about too much again. I felt another swift blow to my face, this time tasting the metal tang of my own blood. I refused to give him the satisfaction of thinking he hurt me. "Well, you know what they say," I said, as I wiped my mouth on my shoulder, "Men who beat on women are clearly compensating for greater inadequacies."

As I braced myself for the next blow, I heard a gun shot. With my ears still ringing, I whipped my head around and saw Thomas. He was halfway down the staircase. His gun was pointed directly at my attacker. The door to the tiny room flew open and Thomas shot that man too. Twice. Once to the body and once to the head. I felt paralyzed. I looked down at the distorted body crumpled at my feet, the syringe still in his hand. I looked up at Thomas as he swiftly descended the staircase. I was thunderstruck. All I could do was gape as Thomas approached me.

"Let's get you out of here, shall we?" he said.

I could only nod. Thomas walked behind my chair, bent over to untie my arm restraints. I rubbed my wrists as he made his way to the front of the chair and untied the ropes that bound my legs. As he stood up, our eyes made contact and held for a moment before tears began to streak down my face. He held out his arms to me. I stood up and wrapped my arms around his neck as tightly as I could. His embrace felt so warm, so comforting. Despite everything, I just needed to feel safe – if only for a moment.

Thomas embraced me for another minute before letting go.

"Frankie, we must hurry," he said.

I looked down at the man on the floor.

"He was going to kill me," I said.

"Frankie, look at me," Thomas said, gently taking my arm. "We have to leave now."

I looked up at Thomas and nodded. He held my arm as I stepped over the man on the floor. I looked down again. His eyes were still open. It sent a cold chill up my spine. It was as if I had touched death itself.

"Frankie, let it go. We must hurry."

Thomas and I made our way up the stairs, out a side door and into a waiting jeep. The engine was still running. He helped me into the passenger seat, then ran to the other side of the vehicle and hopped in. Thomas put the jeep in reverse, threw it back into drive and spun out of the driveway, kicking up a great deal of stones in the process.

We drove at an incredible pace through the landscaped hills and onto a highway. I began to rub my wrists again, then looked over at Thomas and said, "Am I finally going to get some answers?"

He glanced over at me and said, "Yes, you are. But first take these tissues. There's a bottle of water behind you. As quickly as you can, wash your face. There is also a clean shirt in the bag behind the seat. We have to get somewhere safe, then we can talk. This has now become much more complicated."

CHAPTER 29

Thomas pulled into the Orebro airport about fifteen minutes later and parked the jeep as close to the front doors as he could.

"Where are we?" I asked, looking around. I knew we were at an airport, I just didn't know which one.

"Orebro airport," he replied.

I got out of the jeep and looked around, then something occurred to me. "Thomas," I said, turning around to look at him.

"What is it?"

"I don't have my purse. My passport is in it."

"I have made provisions," Thomas said, as he made his way towards the back of the jeep. "Please do not worry."

I leaned up against the side of the jeep and rubbed my temples.

"How far are we from your apartment?" I asked.

"About half an hour."

"I don't remember a thing," I said, more to myself than to Thomas.

Thomas took two small suitcases out of the back of the jeep and led me in the direction of the airport. We followed the signs that read, *Avgångar*, or *departures*, he explained.

Before entering the airport, Thomas took me by the elbow, turned me around, looked me square in the eye and said, "Do not ask any questions yet, just take this, and do not over-react, please. There are cameras everywhere."

He handed me a passport with my photo on it and a name that read, Gillian Brookes, birth place, England, UK. I stared at the passport for a moment then casually tucked it into my pocket and turned towards the entrance doors.

"How are my bruises?" I asked.

Thomas turned towards me to inspect my jaw line.

"They are still just red. When we get inside, we will find a shop and purchase some make-up for you."

As we approached the first ticket booth, Thomas brushed gently passed me, took my hand and said to the gentleman behind the counter, "Two tickets to Antalya, Turkey, please."

He squeezed my hand begging me not to react. He looked at me and smiled. I smiled back, trying to keep the bruised side of my face away from the ticket agent's line of sight. After all the formalities of showing our passports, checking our luggage, and answering a few questions about our journey, which Thomas obviously handled, we set off towards our departure gate. On the way, we found a shop that carried a modest supply of make-up and purchased some taupe-coloured oil-based foundation, which I applied immediately.

Within thirty minutes, we were settled on the plane, buckled in, and taxiing down the runway ready for takeoff. As the Fokker 50 thrust itself into the air, Thomas turned to look at me and said, "Okay, this is going to take a while to explain. I hope you are ready for this."

For a second, I think he contemplated holding my hand, but then changed his mind. I think it was the look on my face.

CHAPTER 30

"Where would you like me to begin?" Thomas asked.

The sense of fright I had from being kidnapped was diminishing rather quickly. In fact, it was now turning to anger. I felt like I had been pulled from pillar to post, without warning, without consent, and it seemed Thomas was about to receive the brunt of my resentment.

"Let's start with who the hell you really are, shall we?" I said, my voice dripping with venom.

"What do you mean?" he asked. "I have already told you."

I glared at him and said, "Okay, let me see your passport."

Thomas stared back at me. I could see his brain working overtime, trying to figure out how much I knew exactly.

"Let me see it," I repeated.

"Why?" he finally asked.

"Humour me," I retorted.

"I have a feeling I do not have to," he said slowly. "You know already, yes?" It was a rhetorical question.

"Yes, just before I left, I found your stockpile of passports in your other bag."

Thomas stared at me for a few moments before saying anything. I was wondering if he was actually going to tell me the truth, or if he was trying to find a way to back-pedal out of this.

"Thomas Bissett is my real name. I use the other passports when I have to. It is the nature of the business I am in."

"And what business is that exactly, Thomas?" I asked.

"I am in intelligence work."

"Oh, god, I am dating James Bond!" I spat, not caring how sarcastic I sounded. "You're a spy?"

"No, I am an intelligence officer. There is a difference."

"Like what? You didn't get the Aston Martin?"

"That is very amusing."

"Why didn't you tell me?"

"I could not."

"Am I under some sort of investigation?"

"Yes, but you are not the prime target. That would be your father," he explained.

"So you thought you'd get to him through me?"

"Yes, something like that," he said, his eyes searching mine for any sign of understanding.

"How did you know where they took me?" I continued.

"Those men work for the same organization I do."

"Charming."

"Okay, Thomas. You'd better start from the beginning, and I swear if you leave anything out, you will regret ever knowing me."

I think I saw him grin.

Thomas reclined his seat a bit and urged me to do the same. After the flight attendant brought us the coffee we ordered, Thomas looked at me and said, "Please, Frankie, first tell me the last time you were in touch with your father."

"I was still a little girl," I said.

"Not since then? This is the truth?"

"Yes, Thomas. He was a bastard. He left when I was still quite young. My grandmother took me to Canada and raised me, Ontario to be exact."

"Are you aware of whom your father really is?" he asked carefully.

"Unfortunately, I know he is, or was, heavily entrenched in the Polish mafia, but that's all I know. Why?"

"He has created quite a situation for himself. Yes, you are correct. He was very high up within the Polish mafia, but only up until a couple of months ago. There was a new coalition forming between the Polish mafia and Bulgaria's Red. Your father did not want the amalgamation to happen and was quite vocal with his opinions. The leaders of each of these organizations joined forces and tried to eliminate him, seeing his dissension as an undermining force and impediment to a more powerful organization. What they did not expect was for Józef to retaliate and become an informant for Interpol."

"What! That is crazy. There is no way," I said, shaking my head.

"Why do you say that?" Thomas asked, as he stirred some more cream into his coffee.

"My father? Cooperate with the authorities? Especially the international police? I find that very hard to believe. I may not have known a lot about my father's business, but I can promise you this. He had no respect at all for the police, or for the government for that matter."

"Actually, you are quite correct," Thomas said. "He did offer Interpol a lot of inside information, but he turned on them as well."

"You've lost me, Thomas," I said, starting to feel my headache coming back again.

"Let me start from the beginning, yes? After Józef openly protested the merger, there was an attempt made on his life. He knew who was at the core of it, or at least he knew the order came internally. Your father still had a lot of people loyal to him within the organization, and he did his best to rally those individuals in an attempt to thwart the unification, but it was to no avail. The amalgamation went ahead as planned. Józef felt exceedingly betrayed. He went underground for a few weeks before getting in contact with Agent André Bruyere."

"That's the agent who was murdered."

"Yes. The agency sent you the link to the newspaper clipping," Thomas explained.

"Why?"

"It was all about your reaction," Thomas said, holding up a hand and motioning for Frankie to be patient for a minute. "Please let me continue. About two years ago, Józef had some business in Amsterdam. The associate he met with there introduced the two of them. Bruyere has been dirty for a long time. He had been under internal investigation for quite sometime, but they could never pin anything on him. Actually, I think the reason Bruyere took as many chances as he did is because he knew he was under investigation and no longer cared. Anyway, Józef worked with Bruyere on several occasions. I do not think he ever fully trusted him, a man like Józef would not, but he liked what Bruyere could bring to the table. Then another drive-by was attempted, but this time it was not directed at Józef, it was directed at his wife. And they succeeded."

"Józef remarried?" I asked, taken aback. "And, she was murdered?"

Thomas looked at me and said, "Yes."

He waited for me to say something, but I simply sat back in my seat. I wasn't surprised someone married to Józef was murdered. I still felt he murdered my mother. I didn't know why it bothered me that he remarried. I guess for a split second I thought about him showing interest in someone other than his own family. Well, his first family that is. But then I remembered who I was talking about and realized the poor woman was probably just a pawn in the game. A game that eventually got her killed.

I motioned for Thomas to go on.

"Anyway," Thomas continued. "Józef went ballistic. He contacted Bruyere and they constructed a plan. They thought if Bruyere could bring in Józef Kowalski, *the Józef Kowalski*, then Bruyere might be able to alleviate some of the suspicions that surrounded him, and Józef would be able to take down his former organization in the process. It worked for a while, but only marginally. Interpol still did not trust Bruyere, but they trusted Józef even less, and they were not far off with their suspicions. It was never Józef's intention to turn over a new leaf. He just wanted to see the new syndicate fall. He did some damage to the mid-levels of the new organization by helping to bring down some of the methamphetamine labs and some of the money-laundering connections abroad, but most of the information he provided Interpol with was not enough to harm their primary operations. The new organization may have seen it coming and arranged things accordingly, we do not know. All we do know is they are still thriving. As for Józef, he has gone underground again. And, now with Bruyere gone, he has no connection to the inside, at least as far as we know. We also think he is the one who took out Bruyere after we let him go."

I turned my head towards the window to mull things over a bit. Something just wasn't right, I thought. I excused myself for a moment, squeezed past Thomas and made my way to the lavatories. I walked into the only vacant one available, the one on the right, and locked the door. It was diminutive and dreary but would have to suffice. I looked into the warped piece of tinfoil they called a mirror and gasped. My god, what a mess I was. I splashed some warm water on my face and used the awful green liquid soap they offered to wash my face, hands and arms. The rest would have to wait, I thought. I smelled my armpits and washed them as well. How could Thomas stand to sit near me? I examined the bruising that was now starting to turn colour around my jaw line. I could see I was going to have to apply a few thick layers of foundation again. I leaned up against the vanity as I dried myself with the crisp brown paper towels from the wall dispenser.

"Something is missing," I said to myself. "But what?"

Then it hit me.

CHAPTER 31

I began to make my way back to my seat. Along the way, I bumped into the flight attendant and ordered a glass of red wine for me and a Heineken for Thomas.

I sat down, looked directly at Thomas and asked, "Why do you want Józef?"

"Pardon?" he asked, looking a bit surprised.

"Why do *you* want Józef?" I repeated. "It's a simple question."

"Not only is he wanted for questioning in the murder of Bruyere, but he is also a known Polish mafia boss. It is my job to bring him in."

"There are several flaws in that statement, Thomas," I said. "First of all, Bruyere was murdered *after* Józef had already worked with Interpol. You already had him, or at least Interpol did. Second, he is no longer associated with the Polish mafia, he has been forced out, eradicated, which I am sure came with some sort of deal from Interpol, some sort of asylum perhaps, in return for the information he was providing. Third, none of this explains how Intelligence got involved. Now, back to my original question, why do *you* want him?"

"You have shrewd insight," Thomas said, smiling.

I didn't smile back.

We stopped talking long enough for the flight attendant to place our drinks on our tray before continuing.

Thomas cleared his throat and went on, "We think there is much more he can tell us," Thomas explained. "He is vulnerable right now. We have a lot more resources than Interpol does. We can offer him more. We came on board just after the first attempt on his life. Interpol thought they could handle it. We disagreed. And, since we have a higher authority than they do…"

Thomas left that statement hanging and reached over to take a drink of his Heineken as I thought about what he had just told me. Something still wasn't right. I was going to have to think about it a bit more, but that would have to wait. I had some more pressing questions for Thomas.

"So, how do I figure into the equation?" I asked, sipping my wine.

"As I explained, Józef has alienated himself from both sides. The newly-formed syndicate is still looking for him. I do not think they will miss again. He has nowhere to go, nowhere to hide, at least not for very much longer anyway. This is why you have been under surveillance for the last two months."

Surveillance? Two months?

I was shocked. How could I not have known I was being watched? It made me feel dirty somehow, tainted, almost like I needed a shower. I looked over at Thomas. The light bulbs were now going off in infinite numbers over my head.

"Is this where I fit in Thomas? I was part of your assignment?"

"No, I mean, you were, yes, but you are much more than that now. In the beginning, we knew nothing of you. We did not even know Józef had a daughter, only a son. We stumbled upon that information by accident. We thought he kept you hidden, not so much to protect you, but more to use you as an outside resource. Outside of his immediate world, that is. All that travelling you did. All the places you went to. They were all locations he had connections. Most of the drug cartels were within your reach. It was a perfect way for you to go undetected, a perfect way to assist him. Don't you see?"

"So the antidote to the snakebite is found in the venom, right?"

"Along that type of correlation, yes."

"Well, there is only one problem with that pseudo analogy, Thomas. I was never part of his world. Never. You know for people who call themselves Intelligence Officers, you certainly fall short of your titles," I spat.

Thomas looked at me. He wanted to say something, but changed his mind. A moment or two later, he said, "In the end, our logic dictated that whether you were involved with him or not, he had nowhere else to turn. He has alienated himself from everyone. You are the only one he has left. We thought you were the natural choice, but that does not mean I think the same thing now."

I wanted to be mad at Thomas, but I couldn't, not really. I was furious I was caught up in all this, but it truly wasn't his fault and even though I wanted to blame him, I knew I couldn't. I didn't want to have any part of this mess.

I was getting fidgety and felt like I needed to stand up and stretch my legs for a bit. I stood up and wedged myself between Thomas and the back of the seat ahead of us, then I squeezed past him and out onto the blue-carpeted aisle again. Thomas never said a word. He knew I needed time to gather my thoughts. I walked towards the back of the plane, holding on to the tops of the aisle seats for balance. We were now experiencing some mild turbulence, which didn't help my nerves. I found some standing room just outside of the lavatories, so I decided to stop there. I leaned up against the side of one of the bathrooms. Anything was better than sitting down at the moment. A minute or two later, I heard the click of a lock and watched the lavatory door open and an elderly woman emerge. She was having a bit of difficulty holding on to the door. It was beginning to swing back and forth in the turbulence, so I quickly grabbed it for her. Just as she began to thank me, the chimes sounded and an announcement came over the intercom system asking us to return to our seats.

As I approached my seat I saw Thomas looking out the window, clearly deep in thought. When he saw me, he stood up to let me squeeze past him. I brushed up against him on my way past, and caught yet another whiff of his exceptional cologne. I wondered why scents affected me so.

I sat down and said, "Thomas?"

"Yes," he said, sounding a bit wounded.

"Why did you shoot them?" I whispered. "Those two men I mean. It doesn't make any sense."

He looked at me and said, "Because the agency still thought you were involved somehow."

I stared at him, a thousand thoughts running through my head. Then I realized what Thomas had done. The agency still believed I was involved, but Thomas did not. And now he had completely betrayed his agency, just to save me. That's what he must have meant when he said it was now much more complicated.

"Oh, Thomas," I said. "What have you done?"

CHAPTER 32

We arrived in Antalya just after 6:15 p.m. The airport was bustling with activity, mostly tourists it seemed. The airport was huge, and a lot busier than I had anticipated. Thomas explained this particular airport was the hub for most travellers who wanted to visit the country's Mediterranean coast. It had only been in operation since 1998, he explained, and hosted about ten million passengers a year.

"You're just a walking encyclopedia, aren't you?" I teased.

"It is my business to know a lot about the international marketplace," he said, smiling.

"How could I forget?" I said, rolling my eyes.

He squeezed my hand and smiled.

"Where are we going?" I asked, as we made our way to the baggage claim.

"We cannot stay in Europe," he said. "We have to move on. We will take the next flight to Mexico."

"Mexico! Why Mexico? Why did we come to Turkey then? " I was terribly confused.

"Orebro airport is primarily a cargo airport," he explained. "They only have a small number of passenger flights. We only had Turkey or Crete to choose from. I chose Turkey because I knew it was the first flight out."

"Okay, but why Mexico?"

"I have some connections there. It is where we will be the safest. Once we are on North American soil, we can sit down and figure out what to do next."

"What to do next?" I asked.

"We are now both hunted, Bella. They will stop at nothing. They have already assumed I have told you everything by now. This makes us both immense liabilities. Liabilities they will want to eliminate."

Thomas and I made our way through the masses of people all standing around the now active conveyor belts that would disperse the luggage. After we found ours, we made our way through customs then into the main corridor towards the nearest ticket booth. The ticket agent informed us that the next flight to Mexico left at 10:10 a.m. the following morning.

"Looks like we are spending the night."

"There is a wonderful hotel here at the airport, sir," the agent offered, pointing towards the main exit doors. "Go through those doors and follow the walkway. It leads directly into the hotel lobby."

"Thank you. That is most appreciated," Thomas said, flashing her a brilliant smile.

We walked across the glass walkway and into the main lobby of the Havaalanı Hotel. The circular lobby was very opulent and studded with huge Romanesque columns and baroque mirrors. The floors were Proconnesian marble. A large crystal and brass Aphrodite chandelier hung from the main rafter. Mahogany beams and plush crimson carpets completed its magnificent ambiance. It was truly stunning.

Thomas and I approached the main desk and were informed they still had rooms available. Thank god. I was exhausted.

We paid for our room, in cash, and began to make our way across the main lobby, through some thick glass doors, and into a smaller lobby that hosted the elevators to the upper-level rooms. Thomas pushed the up button on the wall between the two elevators and stood back to watch the illuminated numbers make their way down to the ground level. The one to the left opened first and we stepped inside.

The spacious elevators were brightly lit and heavily decorated with mirrors that stretched from floor to ceiling.

"Charming," I said sarcastically, putting a hand up in front of my face trying to avoid catching a glimpse of myself in them. Thomas squeezed my hand and laughed.

I laughed and pretended to close my eyes. "Tell me when we reach the 8th floor."

Room 813 was just off the elevators to our immediate right. Thomas slid our key card into the security lock that was attached to our door. With one vertical stroke, the tiny light flashed green and we heard the automatic lock click open. Thomas opened the door and motioned for me to go in.

As impressed as I was with the hotel, I was even more impressed with our suite. "Best room in the house, Thomas?" I asked teasingly, as I looked around the room.

"Only the best for you, Bella" he replied, with a beaming smile.

I smiled back, holding his gaze. He had such striking features. His could have been the face that launched a thousand ships, I thought.

Oops. Wrong sex, right concept, I thought. Sorry Helen, no offence.

In the middle of the room, there was a huge canopy bed draped in flowing white sheers with gold appliqués. The white over-sized down duvet and white jumbo pillows looked even brighter against the mahogany wood of the bed. The floor was covered with luxurious oriental rugs and the walls were laden with replicas of famous paintings. My favourite was, *The Bridge at Argenteuil*. Monet painted it in 1874. I think it currently hung at the National Gallery of Art in Washington, D.C.

There was a fruit basket waiting for us on the coffee table and fresh towels were laid out on the end of the bed. Petite pink soaps were placed on top of the maroon towels. The room smelled of jasmine.

As I took in the rest of my surroundings, I caught a glimpse of the phone beside the bed.

"Damn it. I almost forgot. I have to call my friend, Marianne. She is probably going out of her mind with worry," I said to Thomas.

He walked over to me and put a hand on my shoulder, "I am sorry, but you cannot. They will have your mobile phone, and if you have been calling her on it, they will be watching her by now."

"No! Is she in danger?" I asked, desperately searching Thomas's face.

"I do not think so. She has no direct tie to Józef. They will not see her as an immediate threat; however, if we call her now, after everything that has transpired, it will not only raise suspicions about her, but it will also, in all likelihood, allow them to trace the call back to us. I am sorry."

"I thought it was next to impossible to trace a cell phone internationally," I said.

"You would be quite surprised at what the government can do."

Now feeling even more dejected than before, I decided my next destination should be the bathroom, and ultimately the shower. Thomas was busy unpacking his now meagre collection of clothing, while I picked up the room service menu, walked towards him, and tossed it on the bed in front of him. He looked and smiled, "Is that a hint?"

"I'm going in the shower. If the mood takes you, please order us some food. If not, I cannot be responsible for the plants going missing."

Thomas laughed. "Ruffage?"

"Something like that," I said, laughing back.

"Do not worry about a thing. I will order us some food. I would hate to have to explain to the hotel manager that my lover ate the plants."

"Just tell him I'm from Canada, then shrug your shoulders. That would give him something to think about."

"It would do more than make him think," Thomas said. "Bella, they are silk."

We both burst out laughing.

CHAPTER 33

I stood in front of the bathroom mirror and slowly began to disrobe. My body felt like it had gone ten rounds with Sugar Ray. It also looked like it. My hair was dishevelled and my bruises were starting to show through the make-up again. They were coming out in some very interesting hues now. I was particularly fond of the purple. People must have thought Thomas beat me. No amount of make-up could hide these beauties. I cranked on the hot water tap, added just a hint of cold for good measure, and stepped onto its decorative tiled floor. Within nano seconds, I began to feel refreshed again. The therapeutic water sluiced down my naked body like hot oils being rubbed into icy flesh. I was terribly sore all over, but the hot water seemed to have healing powers and began to alleviate some of my discomfort almost immediately. The aroma of jasmine now surrounded me. The fragrance was coming from the tiny pink soap I was using. As I began to lather more of the soap onto the luffa sponge, I heard the bathroom door open. It was Thomas. I didn't say a word. I watched him through the translucent shower curtain. His eyes caught mine and held as he took off his socks, then unbuttoned his shirt. He took his time, our eyes never loosing contact, as he let the rest of his clothes fall to the floor. His naked body was perfect. Thank god he didn't take his socks off last, I thought, laughing to myself. He silently stepped into the shower with me. He took the luffa sponge out of my hand, gently turned me around and began to soap my back.

"Are you terribly sore?" he asked

"I'm fine. Honestly."

He slowly turned me back around to face him. There was regret in his eyes. I started to say something, but he stopped me by softly putting his finger on my mouth.

"Shhh," he whispered, his sweet breath on my face. Staring into my eyes, he wrapped his arms around me and bent his head down to kiss me, as the warm water rained down between our bodies.

CHAPTER 34

Surprisingly, I slept for six solid hours in Thomas's arms before he woke me to say we had to start making our way back to the airport. We only had time for a quick shower and a speedy continental breakfast in the hotel dining room, but both were equally magnificent.

I was feeling quite rejuvenated by the time we returned to the airport, which was a good thing because the flight to Mexico was going to be a long one. Our itinerary consisted of a twenty-hour flight into LAX, with a three-hour layover, then another 6-hour flight to Cancun.

We checked in and were instructed to follow the signs for International Departures and to locate Gate 5, our departure gate. After we found our gate, Thomas meandered off to get us some more coffee, and I took in my surroundings. I love to watch people. I was eternally amazed at how people interacted with each other. Children were sometimes the most fascinating to me.

There was a young lad sitting across from me. He was perhaps three or four. To my right, and down a few seats, was another young lad around the same age. While they continued to amuse themselves with their own individual toys, they were also very aware of each other's presence. Neither of them seemed to care about any of the adults who were occupying the room. They only acknowledged each other. They would stare at each other, or try to catch each other's attention by making loud noises or rolling around on their seats. Every time one of them displayed some sort of action, they would immediately turn to see if the other one was watching. Without caring what anyone else in the room thought, they immersed themselves in their own world of social interaction in its purest form. It was fantastic to watch. They hadn't been tainted by the outside world yet. Thomas's hand on my shoulder snapped me back to attention.

"I am sorry to startle you," he said, handing me my cappuccino latté.

"No problem," I replied. "I was just admiring some social bonding rituals."

"Sorry?" Thomas queried, not knowing what I was talking about.

"Never mind," I said, smiling. "It was just me going off on one of my mental tangents again."

After we drank some of our coffee, I turned towards Thomas, tucked my foot up underneath my leg, and said, "Now that we have some time to kill, please explain to me what happened at Stamford Bridge. Who were those men? Where did they take you? How did you escape?"

"One question at a time," Thomas said, laughing. "The two men who approached me at Stamford also work for the same agency I do. I was supposed to disappear and let them take over surface surveillance."

"Surface surveillance?" I questioned.

"Covert. Peripheral. Not in direct contact," he explained. "They, and by they I mean my superiors, thought I was getting too personally involved. They were, and still are, convinced you know the whereabouts of Józef. I, on the other hand, have been trying to convince them you do not."

"Thank you," I said.

"When I refused to leave the stadium, they decided to take things into their own hands."

"I was so scared when I saw that man hit you," I said.

"I am sorry," Thomas said. "When they took me, I felt as if I had failed you."

"How can you say that? You rescued me," I said reassureingly.

"Yes, but not before they harmed you," he said.

"So how did you escape?"

"I was not truly kidnapped," Thomas explained. "As soon as we left the stadium, and I shall leave out the profanities I threw at them, I was brought back to headquarters and reassigned to another case. I was still kept in the loop about your surveillance. An ally within the agency kept me up-to-date. I knew where you were every minute of the day. Besides, I knew you would be fairly safe as long as you went back home, which was something I was hoping you would do. I should have known you would look for me."

"Yes, you should have. Why would you ever think I would just abandon you like that?" I asked, feeling a bit annoyed by his lack of trust in me.

"I guess I never really thought you would. I was just hoping you would, for your own protection.

"Along with the passports, I also found the photo of Józef," I said.

Thomas froze. It was nice to see that response on someone else's face for a change.

"You did?" he asked, quite surprised.

After a moment, he smiled and said, "I guess I should have known you would go through my bags. Must be that journalistic instinct of yours."

"I wanted to find the truth, to find out what happened to you. I wasn't going to give up."

"That is why they decided to bring you in you know – because you headed for my apartment in Sweden. They thought you either knew more than you were saying, or thought you were going to find out more than they wanted you to. If this was just an affair that went bad, they thought you would have headed straight home. They did not want the hunters to become the hunted," he explained. "By the way, nice work finding my apartment," he teased.

"You shouldn't leave your credit card bills lying around in locked suitcases."

"I have so many more questions, Thomas. Questions I really need answers to. Will you indulge me some more?"

"Yes," he said slowly, but his attention was now focused across the room.

"Thomas, what is it?" I asked starting to get concerned. The look on his face was not good.

"We are being followed."

CHAPTER 35

My first instinct was to look around and survey the room, but I quickly rejected the idea for fear of making eye contact with our follower or followers. I chose to stare at Thomas instead.

"Are you sure?" I asked.

Thomas briefly nodded his head, looked down at his lap, and said, "I am going to have to take care of this."

"How?" I stammered.

"I have to make sure we have safe passage to Mexico, Frankie. I will do whatever needs to be done," he said, now looking directly into my eyes.

I knew he meant it.

I sat back in my seat, staring at him as he began to mentally calculate his next move and quite methodically by the look on his face.

Was this his solution to everything? I wondered. He killed those two agents in Orebro without hesitation and with no obvious regret. He has not even mentioned them. Was this all part of his job? Killing at will and not even thinking twice about it? It was all just too cold for me. I continued to stare at him as I mentally poured over every thing we had been through, every conversation we had had, and every gentleness he had shown me. It was as if he was two separate people.

"No more killing, Thomas, please."

"Frankie. This is not a game. These people will not hesitate to do the same. We have to be the aggressors if we want to stay one step ahead."

"Is that how you live with yourself, Thomas? You take choice out of the equation?"

"When it comes to survival, there is no choice. Like I said, this is not a game. I still consider myself an ethical man. I only do things I have to."

"An ethical man knows he shouldn't, but a moral man wouldn't," I said.

"Then perhaps I am neither, but I can live with that," he replied.

Trying to change his mind seemed to be the equivalent of nailing gelatine to the wall. All I could do was sit back and wait for Thomas to make his next move.

After several minutes, Thomas broke the uncomfortable silence and said, "Come." Then he got up from his seat and held out his hand for me to take.

"Where are we going?" I asked, placing my hand in his and trying not to look or sound distressed.

"We are going to lose him instead."

"Does that mean there is only one of them?" I asked.

"I do not know. It looks like it. I am sure we will soon find out."

We made our way past Gates 1 through 4, in descending order, and out onto the main concourse. There were at least 50 shops we could choose from to get lost in. We started out in a cigar store and ventured towards the duty-free shop. We weaved our way in and out of as many shops as we could and mingled in amongst as many travellers as we could.

"Do not worry. He will not do anything in public, especially in this airport. All we have to do is lose him," Thomas said, trying to alleviate the concerns he knew were running through my head.

"Why especially this airport?" I asked.

"This airport not only surpasses ICAO and ECAC standards, but also has a special security group that is coordinated by their police force – a highly effective system. They also have some of the best detection equipment in the world, including a new-line explosive detection system. These people do not fool around."

As we entered a corner boutique, I turned to Thomas and said, "Well, it's not all in vain. I can at least replenish some of my lost clothing. I truly appreciated the items you brought for me in the jeep, but I can't wear the same two shirts and slacks day after day, can I? By the way, you did very well judging my size."

"It was all in the research," he said, winking at me.

While I was in the change room, trying on pieces of my new wardrobe, Thomas and I devised a plan. Before entering the boutique, we had spotted a lone bathroom a ways down the hallway at the south end of the building. It was located outside the concourse area, so we easily surmised it was the farthest away from everything and everyone. It actually looked like a maintenance washroom, hence we had less of a chance at being disturbed.

After we left the boutique, Thomas gave me a quick kiss on the lips and walked around the corner into a men's clothing shop as I made my way down the hall towards the washroom. I carried all the bags with me. After I walked inside, I placed all the bags on the floor in front of the first stall and closed its door. There were only two stalls to choose from. I quickly stepped into the next stall, stepped up onto the toilet seat and balanced myself. I pulled the door closed, but not entirely, I still wanted the stall to appear unoccupied. A few minutes later, I heard the bathroom door open. My heart was in my throat.

I knew someone was in the room with me, but I did not know where they were or what they were doing. Then I jumped. With a huge bang, the stall door beside me was kicked open. Then, I heard the outer bathroom door open again and a second set of footsteps enter the room. I held my breath. I dared not breathe. My heart was pounding in my throat even harder. Was it Thomas? Was it another one of them? I braced myself for impact. If it was another one of them, I knew it would only be a matter of seconds before they kicked in the door to my stall as well. Then I heard a giant thud. Then nothing. Then some shuffling. I dared not move. An eternity seemed to pass, then a moment later I heard Thomas's voice say, "Frankie, are you all right?"

I stepped down from the toilet seat and opened the cubicle door. Lying on the floor was a man, dressed in a business suit, holding a hand to his head. A small trickle of blood was making its way down his forehead.

CHAPTER 36

Thomas asked me to wedge the garbage can in between the bathroom door and the wall so no one else could enter the facility, while he continued to hold his foot against the man's throat. Thomas released some of the pressure he was placing on it and asked him who he worked for.

No response.

Thomas bent down and patted each of his pockets. He found the man's wallet on the inside pocket of his suit jacket and tossed it to me.

"Who is he?" Thomas asked.

As soon as I flipped it open, I saw his badge.

"He's with EU Intelligence," I said.

I flipped the ID card around and said, "His name is Agent John Rogerson."

"Have to get your bitch to read for you?" The man said flippantly, looking directly at Thomas.

I looked at Thomas. He looked back at me and smiled.

I held the man's ID up closer to my face, then looked down at him and said, "Not very photogenic, are you? Were your parents brother and sister?"

I wouldn't want to repeat the expletive he threw at me. Suffice it to say, Thomas found our modest exchange of repartee quite amusing.

"Frankie, please bring me the brown bag from the boutique."

I picked it up and started to make my way towards Thomas to hand him it to him, but then looked down at the man on the floor and stopped.

"Do not worry. He will not hurt you. If he tries, I will kill him."

The man on the floor looked from me to Thomas. I could tell by the look on his face he believed Thomas's threat.

"What if he has a gun?" I asked.

"Trust me he does not."

"How do you know?" I asked, not truly convinced.

"If he had hidden a gun somewhere on his body, I would have found it. If one still exists, I do not wish to know where."

I cautiously walked over and handed Thomas the bag. With impressive proficiency, Thomas lifted the man up, directed him to the last stall, and began to restrain him with the two belts we bought at the corner boutique. Then Thomas punched the man right across the jaw and rendered him unconscious.

"That is for the bitch comment," he said, rubbing his hand.

"I never believed you could knock someone out like that," I said, totally dumbfounded.

"It is all in the execution," Thomas said. "You have to strike at a right angle and with enough force to sharply twist their head. This will compress the carotid arteries in the neck causing the person to have a minor stroke. They lose consciousness quite quickly."

"Remind me not to make an enemy out of you," I said.

I gathered our bags, which were now strewn all over the floor, as Thomas looked for a way to deter people from entering the facility for a while. We walked out of the bathroom and Thomas put the cleaning bucket and mop we found in the corner of the room in front of the door and wedged a little makeshift sign that read, 'Out of Order' between the door and the doorframe.

"It will not discourage people for long," he said. "Security will check into it as soon as they see the sign, especially when it is written in English. We are going to have to hurry."

We made our way back to Gate 5 as quickly as we could. I was trying desperately not to look nervous. Thomas appeared the epitome of composure, which seemed to be his perpetual demeanour. He always seemed to be in control, I thought, no matter what the situation was. Somehow, I found enormous solace in that. It was as if his mental state was infectious. When we approached our departure gate, we noticed two security guards talking to one of the flight attendants.

"Do you think they are looking for us?" I asked Thomas uneasily.

"I do not know, but we have to make that flight. Either we take our chances with them, or we stay here and get caught for sure."

We approached the gate with much apprehension. I could almost hear Thomas's mind at work. I couldn't think at all. As we walked towards the flight attendant, she looked at us and asked, "Are you Thomas Payne and Gillian Brookes?"

Apparently, Thomas had more than just four passports.

"Yes," Thomas said, handing her our tickets. "Is there a problem?"

"Not any more, sir. Please hurry," she said, tearing the stubs off our tickets and stepping aside to allow us to enter the gate to the plane.

I was very confused. Why were they waiting for *us*? I looked at Thomas totally perplexed. One of the guards noticed my confusion and said, "We cannot allow a plane to take off when there are passengers who are unaccounted for, madam, especially when their luggage has already been placed in the cargo hold. It is a security measure."

"We apologize for any inconvenience," Thomas said. "I am afraid we got carried away in your abundance of shops and lost track of time."

I lifted up the bags in my hand for affect, and smiled.

"That is fine, sir," the other security guard said.

One of the guards said something to the attendant in a Turkic language and then they both left, as Thomas and I hurried onto the plane.

CHAPTER 37

Our plane took off without incident and I began to relax a bit. I was wholly expecting a barrage of security guards to storm the plane and arrest us even before we made it to the runway. I was very grateful I was wrong.

Once we were in the air and could remove our seatbelts, I looked at Thomas and said, "Okay, now what?"

"What do you mean?" he asked.

"Where do we go from here? Other than Mexico, I mean."

"Go?" Thomas asked.

He wasn't understanding me at all. "Thomas, I have spent the better part of a week in total chaos. I have been either chasing after you or running for my life, and now, I am on my way to Mexico. When is this all going to end?"

"Frankie, I know you are tired and confused. I am trying to figure a way out of all this, but I need time."

I sat back in my seat and stared out the window for awhile. There was nothing to see, except a bunch of cumulous clouds beneath us now. I started to pour over everything that had transpired since I left home, but the longer I thought about things, the more frustrated I got.

"I don't understand this at all," I said to Thomas, totally exasperated. "How can a governmental agency take the law into their own hands like this? Isn't there legal protocol they have to follow? What happened to human rights? I mean, don't these people have to answer to anyone?"

"We are not talking about local politics here. There is a hierarchy of government, yes, but there are also levels that supersede those ones."

"You mean they don't have to answer to anyone?"

"I mean they have a different kind of governing body. And, no, they do not have to answer to anyone, at least at the lower levels, as long as they act in the best interest of international security," Thomas explained.

"Carte blanche?" I asked.

"Something like that, yes," he said.

"So who decides what that *best interest* is?" I asked.

"They do."

"So conventional governments have no say or control over them?"

"Most conventional governments either do not know they exist or will not admit they exist. Besides, if the ones that did know admitted to their existence, they would also have to admit to accountability."

I sat there thinking about all this when another thought occurred to me.

"What about the Canadian government?" I asked. "Can't they help me?"

Thomas stared at me for several long moments before answering me.

"They have no jurisdiction outside of Canada," he said slowly.

I stared back at him for what seemed like an eternity. He did not lose eye contact with me, not even for a second. He knew I would put it all together.

"You lured me away from Canada so I would have no protection," I said icily, staring into his eyes.

Thomas simply said, "Yes."

There was nothing else he could say. He turned to face me, "Please understand we thought you were directly involved with your father."

"How did you do it, Thomas?" I asked, ignoring his comment. "How did you get *me* to contact *you*?"

After a brief moment, Thomas said, "I cannot explain that to you. If I did, your life would be in even more danger than it already is."

"Try me," I said adamantly.

"You are going to have to trust me on this," Thomas said, not budging.

I stared at him for a moment and concluded I probably didn't have any choice in the matter. Thomas was not going to explain it to me and, without question, I was going to have to trust him. My life was pretty much in his hands now.

"Fine. Tell me this," I said. "Was that you I was talking to in Lebanon?"

He paused, then said, "No."

"What?" I bellowed.

"Shhh. Frankie, please, if you want some more answers, I would like you to please lower your voice," Thomas said, placing his hand on my arm while looking around. "Please calm down a bit."

"Fine," I said, taking in a deep breath and exhaling slowly. "Who the hell was it then?"

"It was one of my superiors. I was listening in on an extension and recording the conversations."

"Why?" I asked.

"For voice recognition," he explained.

"Voice recognition?" I asked.

"We obtained audio tape of a telephone conversation Józef had with a woman in the United States last month. We speculated it was somewhere near Buffalo, NY. We needed to compare your voices."

"I wasn't in Buffalo last month," I said.

Thomas held up his hand to stop me from protesting while he continued.

"Ever since the North American Free Trade Agreement, US companies have poured into Canada, including a large number of telephone service providers," he explained. "Most mobile phone providers use cell sites, or towers, that only have a range of approximately ten kilometres. That type of phone would have been fairly easy to trace, but this call came from a satellite phone, one that relies on communication satellites to maintain its connections, not towers. These satellites have no borders, so it is hard to pinpoint an exact location. It is not impossible, but it takes time," he said. "We also tried to cross reference that data by targeting the phone's GPS chip, but the phone was turned off before we could extract that information. The closest location we could isolate was Buffalo, and because Buffalo sits right on the southern border of Ontario..."

Thomas let his sentence trail off knowing I could put the rest of the story together.

"And? Was it me?" I asked, staring at Thomas defiantly.

"We could not confirm nor deny it was you."

"Why not?"

"Their phone call only lasted for a few minutes. They were having a disagreement of sorts. We knew an accurate voiceprint comparison between the two of you would be a bit of a long shot because of her elevated voice levels, but we still wanted to try. As a result, we could only connect two acoustic features between your voice and hers. It was not enough. There were also some ambient noise levels in the background. We were able to clear most of those up with noise-reduction algorithms, but unfortunately it was still not enough to provide any additional clarity to the sample for the analysis," Thomas concluded.

"And you were part of it all," I said, looking straight at Thomas. It was not a question.

"Frankie, please. I have already tried to explain this to you," Thomas said.

"And were you ever really in Lebanon at all, *doctor*?"

I didn't wait around for the answer. I got up and marched straight to the back of the plane and into one of the vacant lavatories. I was so mad, tears began to spill down my face – not tears of hurt or anger, tears of pure frustration. I knew deep down inside it wasn't Thomas's fault. None of it was. It was my dammed father's fault. I turned around and looked in the mirror. After a second or two, I sighed. There was no way I was going to let that kind of hatred consume me again. I had already wasted enough of my life being angry. I was tired of it. It took me a long time to figure it all out, but in the end, I knew I was much healthier and happier if I just let things go. I felt as if I was robbed of my childhood sometimes. I never really had the chance to just be a carefree little girl without fear. I guess that fear had eventually manifested itself into resentment which in turn manifested itself into anger. Nonetheless, I wasn't about to let it control me again.

Several minutes later, I returned to my seat. Thomas was sipping a Grand Marnier, straight up, in a snifter, and thumbing through the pages of the duty-free catalogue. I sat down next to him and sighed.

"I have ordered you a glass of your favourite Cabernet Sauvignon," Thomas said soothingly, as he turned a page of the catalogue. "The flight attendant has just gone to fetch it."

"Thank you," I said.

"You were not gone very long," he said, still not making eye contact with me.

"No I wasn't," I said, wondering why he had made such a peculiar statement. "Why?" I asked.

"I was just sitting here calculating how long it would take someone to recruit a lynch mob. I gather you did not have enough time to do so," he said, barely holding back his grin.

I started to laugh. I couldn't help it.

"I'm sorry, Thomas. I know this is not your fault. If anything, you have been my protector through all this. Please forgive me."

"There is nothing to forgive. You have been tossed into an unknown situation. It is perfectly within your right to feel thrown off balance," Thomas said soothingly.

"Does anything ever upset you?" I asked, as my wine was set down in front of me.

"Yes," he said, promptly pointing at one of the pages in the magazine. "It is just appalling that her shoes do not match her handbag."

I had no recourse but to hit him with the magazine.

I decided to give Thomas a break from my incessant cross-examination efforts so we could watch the in-flight movie. I was finally starting to relax, again.

Thomas took my hand in his, we reclined our seats, and propped up our pillows in an attempt to get comfortable in our 2 x 2 seating spaces.

"Why can't they make these seats more comfortable," I complained, while wriggling around mine.

"Relax. After the movie, I have plans for you," Thomas said, smiling.

"Really? What plans?"

"I believe it is referred to as the mile-high club," he said, beaming.

"You are joking, right?" I asked, smiling back at him.

"It is going to be a long flight, Bella. I do not think I can be without you for that long," he said, kissing the back of my hand.

"To hell with the movie," I said. "I'll see you in two minutes. The one on the left."

I got up and made my way to the lavatories near the back of the plane, praying the one on the left would be empty.

Thirty minutes later, we returned to our seats one after the other with enough inconspicuous time in between as not to draw any attention to ourselves. It didn't work. Everyone seemed to notice. It could have been our imaginations, but Thomas and I laughed just the same. We laughed even harder when every time the flight attendant spoke to us, her sentences seemed to have a *double ententre*. After our laughing diminished a bit, we snuggled up with each other to watch the rest of the movie. They were showing, *Pirates of the Caribbean II*. As Johnny Depp's face filled the screen, I thought, "Now there's a realm of fantasy I wouldn't mind entering into – but only if you wear the pirate costume, Johnny," I said to myself, then laughed aloud.

"Did I miss something?" Thomas asked, looking over at me.

"Sorry," I said. "It's nothing."

Then I laughed again. I was going to have to stop doing that.

CHAPTER 38

After the movie was over, we were served a fairly decent meal of grilled tilapia, wild rice, steamed broccoli and a garden salad with raspberry vinaigrette dressing. We were also given a crusty roll with our meal, but mine mysteriously disappeared when I went to the lavatory.

During dinner, I asked Thomas why he thought Józef ordered the hit on Bruyere. I smacked him when he rolled his eyes at me.

"Can we please have at least one hour together when you are not grilling me for information? I am beginning to feel like I belong on a witness stand," Thomas said, smiling.

"Very funny," I replied, discounting his comment. "Why do you think it was him, or at least his men?"

"I just do."

"How?" I asked impatiently.

"I just do."

"Tell me how?" I said stubbornly.

"Why?"

"Can you please stop with the ambiguity? Thomas, I need to know what happened."

"We inadvertently set Bruyere up."

"What do you mean?" I asked.

"We knew he was involved with Józef, but he did not know that we knew. We specifically requested him. We recruited him to follow you saying we needed an outside source for surveillance. His job was to follow you and report your movements, including whom you met. He was never supposed to be at Gatwick airport. That was an internal error on our part. As a result, I could not meet you there, because I knew he would recognize me. Additionally, *you* were never supposed to notice him there. In fact, you have hindered a few of our plans, but we will leave those to discuss another day," he joked.

"Anyway," Thomas continued. "We sent him to the beach earlier that morning and told him where to position himself. We did not tell him this, but you were supposed to see him, at least we hoped you would. We positioned him fairly close to the path. I was supposed to return to our room and suggest you take a stroll along the beach, straight past where he was standing, while I took care of some alleged business calls. We did not expect you to go for a run. You inadvertently did all the work for us. We had to move quickly.

"Why was I supposed to see him?" I asked, vaguely confused.

"If you were truly connected to Józef, you would have probably met Bruyere at some point. When you saw him you would have been surprised, perhaps even approached him. You would never have guessed you were being watched. Ultimately, we were trying to gauge your reaction when you saw him. Several eyes were upon you that morning."

"Were you watching me too?" I asked.

"For right now, I am going to lie to you and say, no, I was not. You can shout at me later. For now, let me finish the story," he said.

"You think that charm of yours will get you anything, don't you?"

"Yes, I do," he said, smiling.

"Anyway," he continued. "We were the ones who staged his kidnapping. We wanted to push the envelope a bit more, so to speak. Everything was all set up to see how you would react. We dropped him off in Folkestone where there was a car waiting to take him to London."

"Okay, so now you know why I reacted the way I did, but how does Józef factor into all this?" I asked.

"Unfortunately, we are now quite certain Józef had him followed, something we did not factor into our plan. Once Józef found out that Bruyere was also working with Intelligence, his first conclusion would have been that he was being set up."

"But this is all just based on supposition," I said.

"Not all of it," Thomas said carefully. "Bruyere was also found with his knee caps blown off and his tongue cut out and shoved down his throat, a little something the newspaper was never informed of."

I sat back and tried to absorb everything Thomas had just told to me. I felt sick to my stomach. How could I be related to such a monster? Thomas must have sensed what I was feeling.

"Do not be concerned, Frankie," he said, in a low whisper.

"It's not that, Thomas," I said. "I just can't believe what a monster he is."

I felt my stomach drop and my knees go weak. My hands instantly broke out in a sweat.

"Thomas!" I said, spinning my head around to look at him again. "If Bruyere was on the beach watching me, and Józef's men were watching him, they would have seen me as well. Now he knows where I am, or at least where I was," I said, trying to steady my voice.

"You do not have anything to worry about. Those men would not know you. They were not privy to what we were doing, they were only suspicious that Bruyere might be working for Intelligence. That is all. He was merely followed to Hythe. He never had the opportunity to tell Józef what he was doing. Your name would never have been mentioned. I am sure of it."

"I hope you are right, Thomas. Because if Józef thinks I am involved, he will not tolerate that kind of betrayal. He will track me down and he will kill me."

CHAPTER 39

For the duration of the flight, Thomas and I either slept, ate or talked, which was pretty much all you could do on a plane. We had sort of an unspoken pact and avoided talking about any subject matter that included intelligence, espionage, or my father – something I was extremely grateful for. I think Thomas was too.

When we finally arrived at LAX, Thomas and I decided to make the most of our three-hour layover and take in some of the sights in the immediate vicinity of the airport.

"Where do you wish to go?"

"Let's go for a drive along the Pacific Coast Highway."

And that is exactly what we did. We walked through the front doors of the airport, hailed a taxi, and jumped into its backseat.

"Where to?" the driver asked, looking at us through his rear view mirror. He was wearing a Lakers cap and looked in bad need of a haircut. Uneven tuffs of grey hair were shooting out in all directions from underneath his cap.

"Just for a little drive up the coast, please, but not too far," I said. "We have another flight to catch in three hours."

"Well, Venice Beach isn't too far. It's a very popular tourist spot," he offered, now turning around and hooking his arm across the back of his seat.

"It sounds too busy for me," I said. "We just want to catch a bit of sun and go for a bit of a stroll before we are stuck on another cramped airplane."

"Marina del Rey?" the driver suggested. "It's not too far and you'll probably find a nice quiet spot to relax."

"Sounds good to me," I said. "Thomas?"

"What ever you wish, Bella. Any distraction would be very welcoming right about now."

We drove out of the airport onto North Sepulveda Boulevard and immediately merged left onto Lincoln Boulevard. We drove through three little communities along the way, Westchester, the Ballona Wetlands and Playa Vista, until we came to Bali Way. Our driver turned onto Bali Way, pulled over and pointed us in the direction of the marina, which was literally just a stones' throw away. The whole trip took less than ten minutes.

"That was quick," I said.

After we paid the cab driver, we got out of the cab and started to make our way towards the waterfront.

"It's a good thing we got American currency and not Canadian at the exchange booth," I said, laughing.

"Why is that, Bella?" Thomas asked.

"The Americans sometimes refer to Canadian currency as Monopoly money," I explained.

"Monopoly money?"

"Colourful and looks nice, but not worth very much."

"Ah," Thomas said, laughing

When Thomas and I reached the harbour, we looked around and decided to take a stroll down the first path we found. We walked very slowly along the water's edge, taking in as much of the scenery as we could as the mild ocean breezes blew across our faces. I licked my lips and could taste a brief hint of salt on them. When we reached the end of the footpath, I leaned up against one of the half-walls and tilted my face towards the California sun and smiled. I opened my eyes and looked around. I spotted some surfers just down the beach.

"Look, down there," I said, pointing.

I had always wanted to learn how to do that, I thought. There just weren't a lot of places to surf in Southern Ontario.

"Something you aspire to learn?" Thomas asked.

"Okay, get out of my head," I said, laughing.

We walked back towards the marina and found a picnic bench to sit down on. We watched the pelicans and revelled at their collaborative efforts to steer the smaller fish they coveted into shallower water before scooping them up in great numbers into their beaks. We also tried our best to catch a glimpse of any grey whales that may be swimming off in the distance. Unfortunately, we had no luck with that endeavour. Thomas and I had read a sign along the footpath that informed us the grey whales made their way past Marina del Rey as part of their yearly thirteen-thousand-mile-long roundtrip migration journey from the Alaskan seas to the lagoons of Baja where they went to deliver their calves.

We sat on our park bench until Thomas informed me an hour and a half had already gone by and we would have to start making our way back to the airport soon.

"Let's just walk a smidgen more, then we'll head back," I said, taking his hand in mine as I stood up from the picnic bench.

A bit farther up the path, we stumbled upon Fisherman's Village. It was the hub of the Marina del Rey community and their prime shopping area. I smiled.

"You did that on purpose," Thomas said.

We didn't have a lot of time to look around at Fisherman's Village; but, I was able to purchase one of my favourite eau de toilettes before we began to head back to LAX. I sprayed a bit on my wrists as Thomas and I made our way back to Bali Way to look for a taxi. I waved my wrists in the air for a moment then held one up to Thomas's nose for approval.

"Yes, very nice," he said.

There were several taxis waiting when we got to Bali Way, so we jumped into the one at the front of the queue.

"LAX departures," I said to the driver. This time it was a woman.

"Heading anywhere nice?" she asked.

"Mexico," I said, smiling.

"Wonderful," she replied, and turned her attention back to the road in front of her.

When we entered the airport, through the automatic sliding doors, I turned to Thomas and said, "You see? When you smell this good, doors automatically open for you."

Thomas laughed and shook his head at me.

That was pretty much the same reaction everyone gave me.

CHAPTER 40

We had to briefly pass through security again because we ventured out of the airport, but we were not detained too long. I guess they were used to people with lengthy layovers leaving the facility, but the brevity of it all was still a bit surprising to me. Homeland Security's procedures usually took a lot longer than that, but I guess because we had already gone through international customs, going through local security was a bit less strict.

Compared to our flight to Los Angeles, our flight to Cancun went by in a flash. They served one light meal just after take-off, showed a movie starring Will Smith and his son, and about an hour before we landed, we were served cocktails and a snack. I concluded very quickly red wine did not go well with cheese-filled pretzels.

As we began to make our descent, I started to get that ominous feeling in the pit of my stomach again. Our last flight was almost over, and I was rapidly beginning to lose the thirty-thousand-foot buffer zone that had given me enormous comfort over the last thirty hours. We touched down with just a little bump and began slowing our speed at an impressive rate. Before we knew it, we were docked and secured. Thomas got up first and retrieved our shopping bags from the overhead compartment. We had not spoken in the last twenty minutes, other than me complaining again about the aftertaste in my mouth from the pretzels and wine.

I wondered if Thomas was feeling the exact same way I was. Worried. As we departed the plane and made our way through customs, I unconsciously scanned the airport, carefully watching all the people in it and looking for anyone who appeared suspicious to me. Funny how quickly things change, I thought. I used to watch people for fun, not as a survival exercise.

Thomas took me by the hand, nudging me back to attention and said, "After we find our bags, we will have to hire a car."

"Where are we going?" I finally asked.

"Merida."

We exited the airport and found the nearest car rental outlet we could. We rented a black Passat, drove out of the airport and began to make our way towards the *carretera de cobro*, or *toll highway*. Once we hit the highway, I looked at Thomas and said, "How long a drive is it?"

"As the crow flies, about two hours. For us? Probably four."

"You purposely waited to tell me that," I said accusingly, but with a smile on my face. "You knew once you had me in the car, I would not be able to protest as much. You thought I'd just resign myself to the idea of another lengthy trip?"

"Guilty as charged. And yes, I was saving that bit of news until now," he said, laughing.

I reached over to adjust my seatbelt and recline my seat a bit more. Then I turned on the radio, found a light rock station that came in clearly, and stretched out my legs.

"I can't feel my backside anymore anyway," I said. "What's another four hours?"

"See? You are resigned."

I punched him in the arm. Thomas looked at me and laughed. He was still laughing at me when our car took the first bullet.

CHAPTER 41

At first, I thought we hit something, but the look on Thomas's face told me a different story.

"Frankie, get down," he said quickly, grabbing my arm and yanking it towards him.

"What the hell is going on!" I demanded, crouching down as far as I could.

I heard several more whistling noises with simultaneous pops as each bullet pierced the metal of the car. How many damn shooters were there? I jumped as one of the bullets hit the side window shattering glass all over us. Thomas swerved to the left, then back to the right trying to thwart their efforts at a clear shot. He was also trying to glance up into the hills on either side of us to see who it was, but his accelerated speed seemed to hinder his attempt to do so. I looked up at Thomas, but he was not about to take his eyes off the road to return my gaze. We skidded around the next bend and onto a straighter stretch of highway. Thomas pushed even harder on the accelerator and we sped off into the distance at what felt like one hundred and sixty kilometres an hour. A few minutes later, Thomas told me he thought it was safe for me to get up. I sat up cautiously and began to brush the bits of shattered glass from the front of my slacks. I turned to say something to Thomas and gasped. He was holding on to his shoulder.

"Thomas!" I screamed.

There was a sea of blood running down the front of his shirt.

We drove for another minute or two, just for safe measure, before Thomas pulled the car over. The red stain on his shirt was expanding. Thomas ripped open his shirt and inspected his wound.

"How bad is it?" I asked with bated breath.

"I think they just grazed the clavicle," he said. "It might have gone right through. I cannot tell yet."

"That's a lot of blood Thomas."

"Not really. It just looks like it. I have had worse, trust me."

Had worse? I thought. "We are going to have to get you to a hospital."

"No. We cannot risk it. It did not strike my axillary artery. I will be fine."

Thomas continued to tend to his wound, wrapping it up with a piece of his shirt he tore off.

"We are going to have a bit of a problem soon," he said. "There are at least half a dozen toll booths from here to Merida. You are going to have to drive while I try to clean this up."

I jumped out of the car, my eyes ever watchful, and brushed as much shattered glass out of the car as I could. I jumped into the driver's seat and began to use a piece of Thomas's shirt to try and wipe off the steering wheel, but it wasn't working.

"We need water, Thomas."

He hesitated for a moment, then said, "I have an idea. Unlatch the hood please."

Thomas got out of the car, bringing what was left of his shirt with him. I popped the hood and got out to see what he was doing. He unscrewed the windshield washer container and twisted his shirt into a coil. He began to dip it into the container allowing his shirt to soak up as much of the blue liquid as it could. He returned to the car and began to wipe off any trace of blood he could find. I watched his face. It was as if he was in no pain at all. Then I saw him wince as he stretched to the other side of the car. Ah, I thought, he was human after all.

The washer fluid worked like a charm.

"It cut right through the blood," I said. "It can't believe it dried so quickly."

"That would be because of the methyl alcohol," Thomas explained.

When we were finished wiping everything off, Thomas ditched the wet fragments of his tattered shirt into the bushes at the side of the road, took a clean one out of his bag, and settled back into his seat to check his wound again. He lifted the makeshift bandage up and gently patted at the wound, then put it back down and applied more pressure to it. It looked like the bleeding was starting to subside a bit, so I felt slightly better about it. I fastened my seatbelt, turned the engine over, and began to head in the direction of Merida. The first toll booth was less than a few minutes down the road. Once we made it past that one without incident, I was able to breathe again.

"Thomas," I finally said, "They found us. How did they know?"

"I am not sure," he replied. "I was not expecting to be found just yet. As soon as we get to Merida, I will find out."

"How?" I asked.

"Please, Frankie."

That was all he said. Apparently, he did not wish to discuss it any further, so I decided to drop it. For now.

We drove along at an easier pace for the rest of the journey. It was not as bad as I thought it was going to be. Each time we passed a toll booth, the attendant did not seem to pay any particular attention to us. They just concentrated on collecting their tolls, which made sense, I guess. It wasn't as if we were going through border patrol. The final booth was a bit more problematic though. For some reason, the attendant began to question Thomas about something, and

Thomas answered him accordingly – in Spanish. Was there a language he didn't speak, I wondered? Oh, right, none of the Turkic ones.

I did not understand a lot of what they were saying, but I definitely recognized *policia* and *problema*. All I could do was hold my breath and hope for the best. I listened as intently to the conversation as I could, but the attendant was now speaking so fast, I could barely understand anything at all. A moment later, Thomas looked at me and said, "We need to pull over to the side of the booth."

I cranked the wheel to the left, pulled up beside the toll booth, and turned off the engine. Thomas got out of the car, asked me to stay where I was, and walked over to speak with the attendant. Through the side view mirror, I watched as Thomas approached the man. There was an exchange of more words, then Thomas walked into the booth with him. I could not see where he was or what he was doing. I didn't know if he was all right or in trouble. I didn't know what to do at all. Should I stay in the car as Thomas requested, or should I go and see what was going on just in case he needed me? I decided to wait a little bit longer. While I stared diligently at the side view mirror, praying Thomas would walk out of the booth unharmed, he did. He walked straight back to the car, got in and said, "Please drive."

I turned over the engine, put the car in drive, and pulled out onto the highway again.

"Are you all right?" I asked, wiping a bead of sweat from my forehead. "What happened?"

"There is an accident up ahead. The police are directing people around it. There are several different routes we can take through the smaller towns. The attendant showed me on a map."

"That's it? That's what this was all about? You could have said something to me," I scolded him. "I was scared to death!"

"I am sorry, Frankie. I was concentrating on trying not to give away the fact I had just been shot."

I looked over at him. "Sorry," I said softly.

Thomas looked at me, but did not say a word. His response took me by surprise for a moment. Normally he would have brushed it underneath the carpet, so to speak, then laughed.

I turned my head back towards the road, but in the process, something caught my attention. I glanced back at Thomas's left hand. There was fresh blood on it. I looked at his shoulder. There was no new blood. I glanced back at Thomas's left hand, then I looked up.

Thomas was staring straight at me.

CHAPTER 42

"Problem?" he asked, his eyes not leaving mine.

"I was just hoping the bleeding hadn't started again," I stammered, trying to avert his gaze.

Thomas looked down at his hand, then back at me.

"Perhaps it is still bleeding," he offered.

But, I had that bad feeling in pit of my stomach again.

We drove in silence until we reached Highway 18. From there we had to take the detour Thomas spoke of. After winding in and out of a few smaller villages, he said. "Turn left at the fork. It is not too far now."

Fifteen minutes later we passed a road sign that read, *Merida, la Capital de Yucatán.*

As we drove into Merida, I felt as if we were driving into a fantasy world. I had never seen anything like it. It was as if the whole town was painted white.

"It is known as, La ciudad Blanca," Thomas said. "The White City."

"Gee, not hard to figure out why," I replied.

Most of the buildings were constructed out of white limestone, and the ones that weren't, were painted white. The architecture screamed Colonial Mexico. We turned on to Merida's main street, *Paseo de Montejo*, and I was in disbelief. It looked like the Champs Elysée in Paris.

"Have you ever been to Paris?" Thomas asked, as if reading my mind again.

"Yes," I said, looking around. "I can't believe it."

We drove past horse-drawn carriages, palatial mansions, and brilliantly sculpted statues. All the beauty, all the splendour preoccupied my mind for a brief moment, but then I remembered why we were really here. I would probably not get the opportunity to look around this magnificent city at all.

We drove down several other streets before Thomas directed me into the driveway of a lovely colonial home that hosted a three-tiered water fountain on its front lawn.

"Whose house is this?" I asked Thomas.

"My families."

"Your family!" I said, shocked. "Your family lives in England."

"My parents live in England," Thomas said, as he stepped out of the car. "My cousins live here."

"I don't understand something," I said, now strolling over to where Thomas was standing. "If EU Intelligence is looking for us, won't they look in the obvious places first?"

"Yes," he replied, starting to slowly make his way towards the house. "They must have found out we were heading to Mexico. They would have thought about Merida straight away, but they will also have known we are almost untouchable here. I think this is perhaps why they tried to eliminate us just outside of Cancun."

"Why are we virtually untouchable here?" I asked, keeping to his slow pace.

"Merida is the safest place in Mexico, but when you have family here, you are even more protected because everyone knows who you are."

"This is the safest place in Mexico?" I asked.

"There is virtually no crime here. Everyone knows everyone, and there are eyes everywhere. You can take some comfort in the fact that we are reasonably safe here, within limits of course, as long as we do not venture too far."

Thomas opened the front door without knocking, held the door open for me, stepped in behind me, and said, "Hola," quite loudly. A moment later, a young Hispanic lad came around the corner and smiled at Thomas. He had some kind of vegetable in his hand that was dripping bits of soil from its roots as he walked toward us.

"Hola. ¿Cómo está?" he replied, shaking Thomas's hand.

"Hable en inglés por favour. Ella no habla español," Thomas said, nodding towards me.

"I am sorry," he said, now looking at me. "Please forgive me. I will speak in English for you."

I smiled. "Thank you," I said. "I understand some conversational Spanish, but I will try to learn as much as I can while I am here."

He smiled back at me. I think he appreciated my efforts. I always tried to show respect to every culture I encountered.

"Come with me," he said, motioning with his hand, then turning back in the direction he came from.

As we walked through the dwelling, I took great pleasure in its architecture and furnishings. Thomas noticed me looking around and smiled. We walked through the kitchen, through a conservatory and into the backyard. There were several people sitting around a table and a few more working in the garden. As Thomas and I entered the backyard, several of them yelled, "Tomás!" in unison. We walked over to the table and Thomas introduced me. One by one they stood up. The men shook my hand and the women kissed me on both cheeks. I felt most welcome.

One of the women walked over to Thomas and hugged him. He winced. She stepped back and said something to him in Spanish. Thomas replied, then pulled back his shirt a bit for her to look in. She started to speak again, this time her voice was quite authoritative. The woman took Thomas by the other arm and started to direct him into the house. She turned and said something to the crowd. A man and a woman stood up and quickly followed them to the house. Thomas looked back and said, "I will be back soon. Please sit."

The tall, beefy man at the end of the table stood up and motioned for me to sit down in his chair. I did as he requested. An older woman from the other side of the table poured me a glass of what looked to be iced tea, and I sat sipping on it while trying to mentally translate the conversation that was now circling the table. My contribution to the discussion consisted of a lot of smiling and nodding.

It didn't take long for Thomas to return to the backyard. He had on yet another fresh shirt and looked as if some of the colour was returning to his face.

"In and out," he said, looking at me, smiling and pointing to his shoulder.

"Good," I said, smiling back.

Thomas joined us at the table. It was very evident how much he was enjoying his family reunion. In between fits of laughter, Thomas translated most of the conversation for me. I got the distinct impression, though, he was not giving me full details of all of the conversations – details I knew involved me directly.

Later that evening, when Thomas and I were tucked up in bed, I questioned him about it, but he denied ever discussing me with them.

I didn't tell him I knew *novia* meant girlfriend.

CHAPTER 43

Over the next couple of days, Thomas didn't seem quite the same to me. He was ever attentive, yes, but he was also distant at the same time. It was as if he was deep in thought about something. I tried not to let it bother me too much. I thought he could still be a bit off because he was still healing.

One afternoon, I was sitting in the backyard sipping a tea when Thomas strolled out onto the patio to join me. He had just come out of the shower and smelled of Hugo Boss again.

"So, what's the plan for today?" I asked.

"I have to leave for a short time," Thomas said, looking directly at me.

"What do you mean?" I asked, feeling a wave of panic rumble through the hollow of my stomach.

"There is some business I have to see to," he said cautiously.

"And since when does your business not include me these days?" I asked, feeling the edges of anger beginning to build within me.

Thomas did not answer me straight away. He looked at me for a few moments and said, "It might be a bit dangerous. I do not want you in harm's way. You will be much safer here. If I do not have to worry about you, I will be safer as well."

"Where are you going?" I asked.

"Tulúm. I will be back in two days."

"Why?"

"I have to meet with some associates."

"Who?"

"You do not know them," Thomas said. "Frankie, please do not be angry. I wish only to keep you safe."

"Fine," I said. "I'll be here."

I stood up, picked up my tea, walked into the house, up the stairs and into our bedroom. About half an hour later, I heard an engine turn over and walked towards the bedroom window to see who was leaving, not that I didn't already know who it was. I saw Thomas in the front seat of the black Passat. As he pulled out of the driveway, he stopped and looked up towards the window. Our eyes held for a moment, then he sped off out of the driveway.

"I see you had the car window fixed rather quickly, Thomas," I said softly, to myself. "Exactly how long have you been planning this little trip of yours?"

That evening, I went to bed early trying to think of *my* next move. Thomas seemed to be in control of everything at the moment, and that wasn't a feeling I was quite comfortable with anymore. First, he hadn't been acting like himself and now he had left me behind and refused to tell me who he was meeting with. Did he find out who was shooting at us? The whole thing just didn't sit very well with me.

I started to feel exhausted. I resigned myself to the fact that I couldn't go anywhere tonight, so instead I decided to get a good night's sleep and deal with my situation from a fresh perspective in the morning. So, I had a quick shower, tucked myself into bed, rolled over and turned the lamp off. I was at least grateful for the fact that our bed was exceptionally comfortable and would help me get a good night's sleep.

I must have slept for quite a while because it was only the slightest noise I heard downstairs that woke me. I usually slept like the dead. Then I could have sworn I heard Thomas's voice, so I sat up in bed and checked the clock on his side of the bed. It was 4:53 a.m. I listened as carefully as I could, but there was nothing. Then I heard a door close and more muffled voices. They seemed to get louder. Were they having an argument? I stood up, wrapped my silk turquoise housecoat around me and opened the door a crack. There was definitely a heated discussion going on, but I couldn't make out who it was or what it was about.

A moment later, I heard a door open and someone begin to make their way up the stairs. I closed the door as quietly as I could and hopped back into bed. I jumped as the door to our bedroom opened. It was Thomas.

"Frankie, please get up and get dressed. We have to leave. Now."

"What?" I asked, wondering if this was déjà vu or real.

"I have found out who was shooting at us," Thomas said, as he made his way over to the closet and pulled our carry-on bags down from the top shelf. "It was not Intelligence, or at least not directly. Please, I will explain everything in the car. We have to leave now."

"I thought you said we would be safe in Merida."

"We were, but the agency has now upped the ante."

I hurried out of bed and into the bathroom across the hall from our room while Thomas packed our bags. I still had to collect myself a bit mentally, but physically I was ready to go in fifteen minutes. Thomas and I made our way downstairs and out into the fresh dewy air. A dim light that would eventually become a sunrise was already beginning to take form on the horizon. I yawned as I walked over to a deep blue Lincoln MKZ. Thomas was already putting our bags into the trunk.

"What happed to the Passat?" I asked, stifling another yawn.

"Please get in," he said.

Again, I did what I was asked to do without question, an annoying pattern I was tiring of quite rapidly. Thomas was already in the driver's seat before I barely had the chance to close my door. He put the car in reverse and after a speedy three-point turn, we were on our way down the road again.

"Okay, I'm in the car. What is going on?" I said sternly, now feeling a bit more awake thanks to the fresh morning air.

"I am afraid we are in a bit deeper than I originally thought," he said, as he turned onto Highway 180.

"Deeper into what?" I asked.

"I think the agency may have decided to get a bit more creative," Thomas explained. "I think they may have hired an outside source to eradicate us. I do not know how daring these people will be. I suspect they will enter into Merida instead of waiting for us to emerge. If that is the case, I cannot take the chance of putting my family in anymore danger than I already have."

"How do you know this?" I asked.

"I went to Tulúm to speak with some associates, as I told you," Thomas said, glancing over at me. "They were able to access my contact within the agency for me and obtain some information from him. He is a good man. We have been friends for a long time, and I trust him. He used the code word, 'vorsicht.' It means vigilance, in German. It was a private code word between the two of us, just in case the agency was to ever turn on one of us. I do not know for sure what he meant to tell me, but I know he was definitely trying to warn me of an impending confrontation. He knew I was already running from the agency and would be able to predict their tactical manoeuvres, so his warning could only mean they have initiated something a bit more radical. Although it is rare, I have seen them do this before."

"Why do they want us dead? I cannot understand that at all," I said.

Thomas was quiet for a minute. "There is more I have not told you. It is information you asked me about before, remember?"

I thought about it for a moment. There were so many unanswered questions. Then I remembered one in particular, the most recent one. It was when we were on the plane from Turkey to LAX. I asked Thomas how he was able to get *me* to contact *him* on the dating site.

"I remember," I said. "You said I would be in graver danger than I already was."

"Yes, that is correct."

"Well, what is it then?" I asked, impatiently.

Thomas didn't answer me right away. He kept looking intently in his rear view mirror as if he was watching something of significance.

"Thomas? Are you all right?"

"A set of headlights is making their way towards us very quickly," he replied.

"Are they following us?" I asked, as I felt my stomach drop.

"We will have to wait and see. They may just want to pass us."

Thomas kept watch through the rear view mirror, as I turned my attention to the side view mirror. I watched as the truck got closer to us. It was a big red Cherokee with at least thirty-three inch tires and a huge tubular bumper. It was too hard to tell how fast it was actually going.

As the truck approached the back of the Lincoln, it steered over into the opposite lane and began to accelerate. It appeared they were only going to pass us. But just as they were almost parallel to us, they turned the large bumper of their truck into the back quarter panel of our car attempting to put us into a tailspin. Thomas grabbed the steering wheel with both hands trying very diligently not to over correct the spin and swiftly regained control of the Lincoln again.

"What the...!" I gasped, looking around to see where the Cherokee was now.

"Hold on," Thomas said urgently.

He instantaneously cranked the wheel to the left and we skidded off the paved road and across a dirt trail. My hands flailed in front of me until I found something solid in the car to grasp on to. The Lincoln was bouncing everywhere as its tires desperately tried to grip the soft surface beneath us. Twice we hit a pothole and I could feel the top of my head graze the roof of the Lincoln. Thomas twisted and swerved the car, desperately trying to lose the Cherokee behind us. As Thomas began to accelerate, I turned and looked out the rear window to see how close behind the Cherokee was. It was only metres behind us now and seemed to be having significantly less trouble manoeuvring across the soft terrain. The only advantage we seemed to have at the moment was being in front of the dust storm we were creating.

"They are trying to kill us!" I yelled towards Thomas, the sound of both revving engines now exploding in my ears.

"They will try, yes, but they will not succeed," Thomas said confidently, still trying to manoeuvre the Lincoln effectively.

"If I cannot find better ground soon, we are going to have to do this on foot. They have a great advantage over us at the moment."

"On foot? Are you crazy?" I asked, weathering yet another strike into the side of the vehicle.

"If I can just get us to Chichén Itzá, we can lose them in the tunnels."

"The old Mayan ruins? Do you mean the archaeological tunnels?" I yelled, bouncing to the right of the car now.

"Yes, I know them quite well," Thomas yelled back. "They are only a few kilometres away."

Then he said, "Hang on!" and swerved the Lincoln back onto the highway and sped off towards Chichén Itzá.

We heard the Cherokee's engine choke slightly in the sand, but it regained its momentum very quickly. By the time Thomas and I sped into the Mayan grounds, the men in the truck were already only about 50 metres behind us.

Thomas and I abandoned the Lincoln as fast as we could and ran towards the west entrance of the ruins. We heard the Cherokee slide to a halt and then heard two sets of footsteps quickly making their way across the grounds after us. We had no time to look back and see how close they were. Thomas grabbed my hand and we ran at top speed towards the first set of tunnels, purposely knocking down some scaffolding along the way.

"That may stall them just long enough," Thomas said, as we ran into the first tunnel.

We weaved in and out of the tunnels with great efficiency. Thomas knew exactly where he was going, and I could no longer hear the footsteps of the hired killers that pursued us. We scaled two different sets of scaffolding, then sat down on an upper ledge to catch our breath.

A few seconds later, when I could breathe a little easier, I bent over towards Thomas's ear and whispered, "Why have they not just shot us? Why are they still pursuing us like this?"

"My guess is they want us alive, for now," he replied softly. "We should stay here for a while longer. I do not think they will find us here. If they do, we will be long gone by the time they make it up the scaffolding."

We both sat with bated breath as we listened to the echo of the tunnels. We could now hear the voices of the two men somewhere off in the distance.

"Soon they will get frustrated, that is when they will start to make mistakes," Thomas whispered. "When that happens, we will make our move."

Thomas and I sat perched on a dirt ledge just above one of the main passageways. As I looked around, I realized I was sitting in the midst of pre-Columbian history that dated back to 600 A.D. It was an archaeological site I had always wanted to visit, just perhaps not under these circumstances.

I leaned back against the dirt wall and tried to remember everything I had read about it. It was a blatant attempt to distract my mind away from our current situation, but I was also hoping to calm my nerves in the process.

I knew Chichén Itzá was a major city claiming both Mayan and Toltec influences. I remembered that its name literally meant, *at the mouth of the well of the Itza,* and that there were three cenotes, or sink holes, that provided the city with its water supply at its pinnacle of power and population. I couldn't remember how many still existed today, but I knew that one called the, *Cenote of Sacrifice,* was once used as a sacred worshiping site where the Mayans would bring offerings to their god, *Chaac.* I closed my eyes and tried to remember what else was here. I was finally starting to breath normally again.

I vaguely remembered something about the *Temple of Warriors.* I think it sat at the top of a step pyramid, one you could climb from the outside, and honoured the many warriors revered by the Mayan people, but I did not know if I was remembering that correctly or not. I knew there were ball courts that were unearthed here. The Mesoamerican ballgame or, *juego de pelota,* was a sport that encompassed ritual beliefs. Sculpted panels inside the court illustrated some of the beheaded players and captains who played the sport. It was a respect thing. The Mesoamerican people played it for over three thousand years. It wasn't quite modern-day football, but it caught my attention nonetheless.

A direct elbow into my side jolted me back to reality.

"It is time to make our move," Thomas said, as he slowly stood up. "I think they are on the other side of the grounds."

I stood up beside him, carefully balancing myself as I waited for the circulation to return to my left foot. After the prickly sensation subsided, I shook it off and began to make my way back down the scaffolding behind Thomas.

We weaved our way in and out of the tunnels again, back the way we came, until we could see the light to the entrance. The sun was high in the sky now, so there would be no margin for error if we were to be seen.

We inched our way closer to the entrance, listening as carefully as we could for any movement that would betray our enemies' position. We could now see the Lincoln in the distance, but the Cherokee was nowhere to be seen.

"Did they leave?" I whispered to Thomas.

"No, they are still here somewhere. I guarantee it," he said, now making his way to the arch of the entrance.

Thomas glanced outside, then looked back at me.

"If we can make it to the car," he said. "Hopefully we can make it to Tulúm. There is a safe house waiting for us there."

"Do you have a plan?" I asked, continuing to make my way along the inner wall towards Thomas.

"There are only two places they can be," he said. "They are either deep within the other tunnels still looking for us, or they are on the steps directly outside of here waiting for us to emerge. The only thing we have going for us right now is the fact that there are only two of them and four exits to this temple."

"Odds are in our favour," I stated, not at all convinced of what I had just said.

"The only other thing we may need to worry about is if they did any damage to the Lincoln. If they detached any of the engine parts, we could be in serious trouble."

"More serious than this?" I asked, shrugging. "I think that's a chance we are going to have to take."

"I am going to make my way out first," Thomas said. "When I know it is safe, I will tell you. Please, do not come out before I tell you to. This is extremely important."

I nodded. My heart was in my throat again.

As Thomas began to slowly make his way outside, he turned around and looked up towards the steps to the temple. He looked back at me and shook his head, indicating he could not see either of them. He continued to walk backwards, his eyes scouring the total length of the pyramid, as I watched for any sign of movement from across the grounds. Thomas must have sensed we had been given a break, because all of a sudden he turned and began to run towards the Lincoln. Within seconds he seemed to be at the driver's side door. He scoured the area again and motioned for me to run. I ran out the entrance as fast as I could towards where Thomas was standing outside the Lincoln. He was still watching every angle he could. Once I was within a few metres from the car, he jumped in and tried to turn the engine over. The engine let out a horrible sound as it spat and sputtered trying to get the surge of gasoline it desperately needed. I jumped in the passenger seat and begged it to start. Again, all it did was spit and sputter. I looked around waiting to see our pursuers knowing they must have heard the engine by now but still there was nothing. Another second later, I heard the roar of the 8-cylinder engine. Thomas swiftly put the car in reverse to spin us around, then threw it into drive, practically dropping the transmission in the process and peeled out of the grounds towards the highway. I kept my eyes fixed to the rear window until my neck began to throb.

"I still can't see them," I said to Thomas, finally turning around to face him.

Thomas had still not said anything since we left the Mayan ruins.

"Thomas?" I said, looking over at him.

"I do not like this," he said, shaking his head. "Something is not right."

CHAPTER 44

About a kilometre down the road, Thomas pulled the Lincoln over to the side of the road and got out of the car.
"What are you doing?" I asked, following him out of the car.
"I have to check something."
Thomas bent down on one knee, leaned forward and began to inspect the underbelly of the vehicle. I watched as he made his way around the car, performing the same ritual on each side.
"Thomas, what are you doing exactly?"
He stood up and brushed the gravel dust from the knees of his pants. "I was looking for a VTD."
"A what?"
"A vehicle tracking device," Thomas replied.
"I take it you didn't find one?"
"Some are quite small," Thomas explained. "There may still be one, but if there is, I do not know where it is. Unfortunately we do not have the luxury of time on our hands for me to perform a thorough search."
"How accurate are they?"
"That depends on what kind of device they may have used," Thomas began to explain, as he motioned for me to get back into the Lincoln. "The GPS satellite system is controlled by the government. They own and operate the entire entity. I do not think the agency wants this operation recorded or traced. Besides, a GPS tracking device can only track vehicles outdoors. If they did plant one somewhere, it is a safe bet to say it is probably a radio-frequency tracking device. Those ones will transmit right through walls, garages, lower-level parking facilities, etc."

As I sat back down in the front seat, I looked over at Thomas. "So they may be able to track us to Tulúm?"

"Perhaps we will get lucky," he said unconvincingly. "But I cannot see them just leaving like that. One way or the other, I guess we will soon find out."

Thomas pulled back onto the highway and adjusted the rear view mirror to insure an unobstructed view of the road behind him while I kept a vigilant watch on the other areas that were not as easy for Thomas to monitor. We drove in silence for the remainder of the trip for fear of distracting ourselves away from our watch. We seemed to be the only car on the road, which in itself was quite unnerving. It was an ominous feeling that made the hair on my arms stand eternally on end. I knew we weren't far from our destination now. I couldn't wait to be out of this vehicle and into somewhere safe, wherever that was.

Five minutes later, I saw a sign saying, *Bienvenido a Tulúm*, or *Welcome to Tulúm*. Off in the distance I saw a set of traffic lights, which I presumed was the first intersection into the city. I started to breathe a tiny bit easier as we slowed the Lincoln and drove through the lights. I turned my head towards Thomas and asked, "Do you think we are ..."

That was all I could get out of my mouth before the red Cherokee barrelled straight through the adjacent intersection, t-boning the Lincoln and sending us skidding sideways across the soft shoulder and directly into a power pole. The pulverizing impact would have been heard for miles. It was that gut-wrenching, metal-on-metal crunching sound that would have sent anyone within earshot into immediate recoil.

CHAPTER 45

I was the first to come to as I looked around to see where we were and what had happened. The sound of the Lincoln's hissing engine permeated the air as I realized where I was. My senses returned very quickly, completely discounting any fears I may have had as the adrenaline rushed through my veins in an instinctive need for survival. I looked over at Thomas. He was slumped over the wheel, unconscious, I hoped. I refused to think of any other outcome. Thomas's side of the car took the hardest hit. We never even saw it coming. I tried to look out the windshield to see where our attackers were, but it was too shattered to see through. I undid my seatbelt and inched my way over to Thomas to see if he was still breathing, but just as I started to move, I heard someone approach the car. I was still in shock and I knew it. I was trying to think clearly, but that too evaded me. I only had thoughts of Thomas and his lifeless body. I sat as still as I could and braced myself for the worst. I heard a man's voice tell me to get out of the car. I looked over at Thomas and watched his chest for a moment. It took a second or two, but I finally saw it rise up and down, but just barely. Knowing he was still alive gave me the strength to leave the car and face our attackers. I had to be strong. I had to think clearly, for both of us. I pulled myself up out of the seat, through the window, which was now devoid of glass, and rested my backside on the edge of the frame. My head spun as I sat there. I waited for it to subside before swinging my legs out and over the frame and onto the soft ground. As my eyes focused in on the man standing in front of me, I realized he was pointing a semi-automatic weapon straight at me.

"This was too easy," the man said, turning his head slightly, presumably speaking to someone else in the truck.

Another man stepped out of the Cherokee and walked towards the man with the gun. The two of them did not look like hired hit men to me, but then again, I had no idea what hired hit men were supposed to look like. I stood as still as I could, trying to manage the swaying effect now taking over my ravaged body. I was feeling the overwhelming sense of nausea as well and thought for a moment that I might faint. I took a step closer to the front of the Lincoln and leaned up against it, hoping to regain some of my balance.

"All right, let's go," the man with the gun said to me, waving the weapon towards the Cherokee. "Dan, get the other one and put him in the back of the truck. I'll watch this one."

"You can't," I croaked. My throat felt like I had swallowed a bucket of sand. I cleared my throat as best I could and said, "He'll most likely have broken bones. If you move him, he could haemorrhage. He needs medical help."

It was as if I had never even spoken. Neither of them paid any attention to what I had just said. The second man did what he was ordered to do, while I was escorted into the Cherokee by the man wielding the gun. I watched as Thomas was carelessly removed from the mangled Lincoln and dragged by the underarms over to where I was. I watched his face as he was lifted into the back of the truck beside me. He did not look good.

I cautiously tilted Thomas's head slightly, straightening his neck. I surmised I was probably not going to inflict any additional damage, so the least I could do was help him with his breathing. I leaned towards him some more and spoke to him in a gentle voice, "Thomas? It's me Frankie. Please Thomas, say something to me. Please." I stroked his hair and lightly patted his face trying to get any type of response I could out of him, but it was no use. Thomas was deep inside himself trying to heal whatever he could subconsciously. I sat there, carefully leaning up against him wondering where our fate now lied. I was sure we were on our way to our deaths, and there was nothing I could do about it. The two men in the front seat completely ignored us as the Cherokee rolled on heading to wherever it was supposed to be going. I looked down at Thomas, then down at my body. Both were stained with dirt and blood and remnants of other grime I could not immediately identify. I wanted to cry, but I didn't have the strength or the energy to exert the effort. I felt completely numb.

A while down the road, I wouldn't have a clue how long, as I think I too weaved in and out of consciousness, the Cherokee pulled onto a side road and then onto another one before making its way down a long driveway. Up ahead I could see a house covered with white siding. It was quite small and looked more like a cottage than a home to me. The lawn was sparse and looked in bad need of watering, while the trash and litter that adorned the brown bits of grass seemed to be in abundance. I looked around and noticed it was the only house in sight, probably for miles. The Cherokee pulled to a stop in front of it and the two men in the front seat got out. The one called Dan, opened the door on Thomas's side of the vehicle and lifted him half over his shoulder and dragged him out of the truck. I watched as Thomas's head bobbed back and forth, still not showing any sign of consciousness. The driver of the truck stepped out of the way to let his partner pass, then looked at me and motioned with his head for me to get out of the truck. I slid along the seat of the Cherokee and stepped out onto the dirt driveway. I started to walk in the direction of Thomas, but was stopped dead in my tracks as I heard a deep voice behind me say, "Hello, Francesca."

CHAPTER 46

My stomach dropped and my chin fell to my chest. I closed my eyes, but the tears still thrust out from behind them. No matter how hard I squeezed, I could not stop them from emerging. I couldn't move. All of a sudden, I was transported back to another lifetime. I had almost forgotten the hold he had on me. After all this time, it still had not diminished. I had wondered how I would feel facing him again, but it was much worse than I could ever have imagined. Then I heard it again, that voice that compelled me to feel such hatred, such loathing, such abhorrence.

"Are you not going to turn around and say hello to your father, Francesca?"

I gradually lifted my head, looking as far off into the distance as I could. I squeezed the lingering tears from my eyes, as I knew he would see them as an inexcusable sign of weakness and slowly turned around to face him.

He looked much older than I had imagined. If I had never known him and seen him walking down the street, I would have thought him to be somewhat on the frail side. He had lost a lot of weight, at least thirty or forty pounds and was hunched over a bit. He was almost completely grey now and not quite as tall as I remembered, but as he walked closer to me, I saw those eyes – those same eyes that haunted my dreams at night and pervaded my thoughts each and every day. Those eyes that looked back at me knowing I loathed him and taking great pleasure in his control over me. He knew he still had it. Even before calling my name, he would have known how it would have totally shocked me and sent waves of fear though me. He would have known how off guard and weak I would have felt in his presence, never expecting to see him again. He was revelling in it. I could see it on his face.

"It has been a long time, Francesca," Józef said, walking even closer to me. He was using a cane and favouring what seemed to be a bad left knee. He smiled wickedly at me as he made his way towards me, his uneven and yellowing teeth amplifying his evil demeanour. He reached a hand up to touch me, but as soon as he moved, I jumped.

"Francesca, you are not afraid of your own father, are you?"

Our eyes met and held. Yes, he was taking great pleasure in all of this I thought. I had to be strong. I had to pull myself together, but it was so hard. Inside, I was just a little girl again, trying desperately to say and do the right things for fear of angering him. It was the same internal tussle I had my entire life with him. Nothing I ever did was correct, no matter how hard I tried.

"You look a mess," he said. "Come and I will show you where you can clean up."

He reached over to take my arm. I wanted to recoil, but I knew it would make matters worse. As his cold, bony hand gripped my upper arm, I felt as if ice had replaced all the blood within my veins. His malevolence seemed to pervade everything around him. It was a presence I never knew anyone could have. That was the kind of feeling that swept over you when you were in his company. It was almost beyond description.

Józef directed me towards the house, into the front foyer, and pointed me towards a closed door I presumed would enter into a bathroom.

"There," he said, nodding his head in the direction of the door.

I stepped away from him, opened the door to the bathroom and stepped inside. Before I closed the door, I located the light switch and lit up my surroundings. My first instinct was to lock the door behind me, but I knew even if there was a lock on it, it would be nothing more than an exercise in futility. It was amazing how every time I was in my father's presence, my primary instinct was to protect myself.

I splashed some warm water on my face and dried it with an old grey towel that was draped over the side of the sink. I put the toilet lid down and sat down to try and gather my thoughts. I immediately thought about Thomas and wondered if he was even alive. I could still picture him slumped over the steering wheel of the Lincoln as I watched his laboured breathing. I needed to pull myself together, find out whether he was all right or not, and find out what Józef had planned for the two of us. I stood up, took in two deep breaths, walked out of the bathroom and back into the front foyer where the driver of the Cherokee was waiting for me.

"Come with me," he said.

I followed him around the corner, through the living room and into another room I thought would be a dining room, but instead it was laid out like an extra sitting room. At the far end of the room, I saw a ratty old brown tweed sofa with Thomas lying on it. I immediately ran to him.

"Thomas? Thomas? Can you hear me?" I was desperately searching his face for any sign of comprehension. As I straightened the front of his shirt and pulled the twisted bit away from his neck, I thought I felt him move slightly underneath my touch, but I couldn't be sure.

"I was a bit surprised to find you hooked up with a federal agent, Francesca."

I flinched. It was Józef speaking. I had not noticed him sitting on the other side of the room. "Are you sure you really know all there is to know about him?"

"What do you want from me?" I asked, turning to look at him, but not taking my hand off Thomas's face.

"Perhaps that is a question you should be asking your boyfriend."

"Well, I would, but as you can see your clever cohorts over there put him in this state, so I can't ask him anything right now can I?"

As soon as the sarcasm came out of my mouth, I knew I should have controlled it. Upsetting Józef was the last thing I needed to do at the moment.

Józef stared at me for what seemed like an eternity. "I see being raised by your grandmother has not taught you any manners."

"How do you want me to react?" I asked, trying to defuse the situation. "I was just run off the road by two of your men, and I don't know if Thomas will even survive it. I'm upset. I hope you can appreciate that."

It was the best I could do. I sat there waiting for his response.

After a brief moment, Józef looked over at one of his men and said, "Get Marta."

As the taller man left the room, Józef stood up. He took a moment to balance himself on his cane, then turned to leave as well. He paused briefly in the doorway and looked back at me. "Do not do anything stupid." Then he limped away.

I turned back around to tend to Thomas when a rather plump-looking woman entered the room carrying a bag with her. She said something to me in Spanish then motioned for me to get out of her way. As she bent down overtop of Thomas, she took out a stethoscope and placed it on his chest.

I watched diligently as she poked and prodded him, but with gentle hands and a soft demeanour. I wondered how she came to be in the company of my father. Could I trust her? I wondered. I tried to say something to her, but all she did was look at me and smile. Either she didn't understand a word I was saying or she wanted no part of befriending me.

When she was through, she looked at me, pointed down at Thomas, and said, "Permítalo dormir."

I knew 'dormir' meant sleep, so I nodded my head in agreement as she turned to leave the room. Once she was gone, I went to Thomas's side again, checked his breathing for my own peace of mind, then looked around the room to try and figure a way out of this. I walked over to the window, while Józef's threat echoed through the recesses my mind. What could I possibly do this far from anywhere? If I did anything to provoke Józef, he would retaliate immeasurably. He had just made that quite clear.

As I turned around to sit down, I heard someone enter the house. I knew it was Józef. I could literally feel his foul presence besiege me again. He walked around the corner, stopped underneath the door frame and stared at me.

"You have changed," he said.

"I am not a little girl anymore. I would have."

"I have seen you as an adult as well."

His sentence shocked me.

"What do you mean?" I asked in disbelief.

"How can I put this?" he said, as he began to rub his chin. Then he walked over to the chair opposite me and slowly sat down, allowing his cane to take most of his weight. "When I allowed Elizabeth to take you, it came with several conditions, including my continual knowledge of your whereabouts."

He allowed that sentence to hover in mid air knowing full well I would never have seen it coming.

"You *let* my grandmother take me? No, she said you left."

"That is just semantics," he said, shrugging.

"I don't understand. Why did you allow her to take me?"

"This comes as a surprise to you, Francesca? We both know you were nothing more than a disappointment to me," he said, matter-of-factly.

I sat there staring at him. I knew he wanted me to react, but I refused. I was used to his insults and malicious tongue. I was sure I could weather a few more.

"What was so disappointing, Józef?" I asked, knowing that calling him by his first name would cut deep into his ego. "The fact that I never wanted to be like you?"

"We both know you would fall very short of that," he said, in a counter attack. "Your brother, on the other hand, turned out to be quite an astounding young man."

"Too bad it got him killed," I retorted, not caring about any backlash anymore.

"Victor left this world with honour, Francesca. Do not besmirch his name. Is that clear?" He was now pointing his cane at me in a jabbing motion.

"So why did you want to know my whereabouts all the time? I mean, if I was such a disappointment to you, why would you want to know anything about me?"

"Do not misinterpret my intentions. I simply needed to know where my collateral was."

"Collateral?" I questioned, frowning at him.

"Your grandmother proved to be quite useful to me on several different occasions. Just after your mother died, Elizabeth began to threaten me. She said she was going to take you away with her. Deep down, she knew it was not possible. She knew I would simply hunt her down and kill her, but that did not stop the threats. I think for that reason alone, I respected her. She was not a weak person. Anyway, you were becoming more and more like your mother everyday. I knew eventually you would be more trouble than you were worth, so that is why I let your grandmother take you."

He paused intentionally. He wanted my imagination to take over and inflict the most amount of damage possible before he continued.

"Let's just say I needed an ally and she willingly obliged."

"My grandmother would never have helped you," I seethed.

Józef paused for effect again. "She would if her beloved granddaughter's life was threatened."

I felt sick to my stomach. "You exploited her and dragged her into your ugly world of corruption and immorality by using me as collateral?"

"No," he said, speaking slowly and glaring at me. "I made an arrangement with her and she agreed freely."

"More like subjugated." I spat.

"Do not get pedantic, Francesca. It does not suit you."

I glared back at him, my mind overwrought with contempt. I felt like I could cry, not for me, but for what my grandmother had done for me. All this time, and I never knew. I held my gaze and promised myself that somehow, I would get revenge.

He stared back at me, then his thin lips curled progressively into a wicked smile. "Do not even think about it," he said, as he left the room.

A moment later, I heard a door close near the back of the house at the same time I heard a slight moan behind me. I spun my head around to look at Thomas and saw his eyes flutter briefly. I ran to him.

"Thomas?" I said, as a smile washed across my face. "Thomas, it's okay. Please speak to me."

"Frankie?" he asked, his eyes still not totally open.

"Shhh. Yes, it's me. Try to whisper, Thomas. We are in a bit of trouble here."

As the words left my mouth, reality hit Thomas and he almost immediately tried to sit up. He winced and moaned again as he realized he was basically incapacitated, at least temporarily.

"What happened?" Thomas asked, reclining back to his original position.

"Thomas, it wasn't the agency after us at all," I began to explain. "It was Józef."

Thomas opened his eyes all the way now and stared at me.

"What?" It was all he could say. I think he was as shocked as I was.

"It was Józef," I repeated. "Those were his men in the Cherokee. We are here, in his house. They are holding us captive."

I could tell Thomas's mind was working overtime. He had closed his eyes again, but I could see the rapid eye movement underneath his eyelids. I leaned back on my heels and studied his face for a moment.

"Thomas?" I said, taking a step back. "What is going on?"

Thomas opened his eyes and looked at me. He wanted to say something but decided against it. He began to shake his head back and forth, his eyes fixed on mine, just as Józef walked back into the room.

I turned to look at Józef and watched him as he made his way to where Thomas was lying. As he approached the sofa, he held out his hand and said, "Hello, Thomas."

Thomas took Józef's hand and shook it. "Hello, Józef."

CHAPTER 47

I was stunned. I stood up and staggered backwards several paces before bumping into one of the chairs behind me. They knew each other? I couldn't believe it. I was so upset I literally turned and ran straight out the front door. I had no idea where I was running to, I just had to get out of the house and away from them. My feet carried me as quickly as they could, and I made it half way across the property before I heard the red Cherokee behind me. I stopped in mid stride. I knew there was nowhere to run. I slowly turned around and started to walk back towards the house resignedly. I thought it was a better alternative than being run down by two buffoons in a truck. The Cherokee idled about ten metres from me and allowed me to make my way back to the house unescorted. Józef and Thomas were waiting for me as I returned. I walked back into the sitting room and stood in the door frame staring at them. Thomas was now sitting as upright as he could, several pillows propped up behind him, and Józef was sitting back down in the chair he sat in during our little tête-à-tête.

"I am glad you have willingly rejoined us, Francesca," Józef said, lifting his cane and motioning with it for me to sit down in the chair across from him.

Without saying a word, I walked over to the chair and sat down.

Thomas was the first one to speak. "Bella," he began.

"Do not call me that," I spat, whipping my head around to glare at him.

I think I heard Józef laugh to himself.

"Frankie, please let me explain," he tried again.

I continued to stare at him.

"It is not what you think. Józef and I are not allies. There is much more to this situation."

Józef interjected. "Trust me, when this is all said and done, I will see to it that Thomas is quite dead. I can assure you." Then he smiled at me through his crooked teeth again.

I looked towards Thomas and waited.

"All of this," Thomas began. "Everything that has happened. Everyone who has been flung together, willingly or not, has all been because of NICO."

Thomas pushed down on the cushion beneath him, trying to sit up a bit higher again before continuing. "The agency has invented a new software program. They call it NICO. The acronym stands for Navigational and Internet-based Covert Operational system."

Thomas paused, perhaps waiting for me to say something. I had nothing to say to him. I believe my facial expression spoke for itself, again.

He continued. "NICO is not like anything anyone has ever seen or heard of before. It is very advanced technology. It goes beyond even the most sophisticated C++ programming languages. This particular software makes spy ware seem almost archaic because it is also completely interactive. They, and by they I mean the agency, are able to navigate through cyberspace virtually undetected."

"What exactly do you mean by that?" I asked.

"In layman's terms, the agency can not only watch what people are doing on the Internet, but they can also manipulate certain programs they are using, while they are using them," Thomas explained.

I looked at Thomas suspiciously, "Manipulate how?"

"First, please let me explain why, I want you to see the whole picture. As a security agency, we constantly need to keep one step ahead of the criminal element. This is very difficult to do, especially when they can waltz through the social order without adhering to any governing rules."

"Unlike the agency," I interjected, sarcastically.

"Anyway," Thomas continued. "The two most prominent issues we have to deal with are surveillance and infiltration. Surveillance only works if you can remain undetected and infiltration can literally take years to establish. NICO was invented to assist with precisely this directive – it combined both initiatives."

Thomas sat up and took a sip of water from a glass now sitting in front of him. He paused for another sip, as I eyed the glass enviously.

"The *how* is a little bit different and twofold," he said. "Primarily, we needed to find the perfect sites to execute the software. They had to be specific avenues where we could pull a surplus of quality information from. We knew the best way to gain a cascade of information from people was to have them volunteer it, so we needed them to be vulnerable. We needed them to feel safe enough to offer it to us and unsuspecting enough to let their guard down. There are only a few isolated places people feel safe and all of them are directly associated with their personal lives. No one can ever completely escape the grid, and there is one place in particular that millions upon millions of people feel as if they are either safe or off the radar."

Thomas finished his last sentence very slowly.

"Do you not see it, Francesca?" Józef said, almost arrogant in his knowledge. "Come on girl, surely you are not that stupid."

There was a pregnant pause, as Thomas looked directly at me. He watched my face very carefully waiting for me to put two and two together. He knew I would feel hurt and manipulated. I was the first one to say it, 'dating sites.'

Józef's cackling laughter echoed through the house. I tried to ignore him and looked back at Thomas.

"Please go on, Thomas," I said bitterly. "I find this very interesting."

I stood up to look out the window. Thomas didn't answer me right away. I could hear him shuffling on the sofa behind me, then clear his throat before he began to speak again.

"Frankie, dating sites were the perfect answer. As I mentioned, people let their guard down. This is why the FBI, the RCMP, and many other organizations use chat rooms to go after sexual predators and child porn rings. People feel untouchable there, anonymous. There are literally millions of people worldwide using these online dating services. It is an informational database of immeasurable proportions."

"I understand predators stalk the Internet," I said. "But why would criminals or terrorists be on a dating site?"

"Do you have any idea how often these sites are used by people trying to gain access to other countries? Our first operation with NICO involved a Sudanese SPLA terrorist who was trying to escape Khartoum. The details are unimportant here, but the bottom line is that we caught him. He was exchanging e-mails with a woman in Washington and trying to use her to get out of Sudan and into the United States. He would never have used conventional methods of e-mail exchange for fear of being traced. So, he used the anonymous method of an online dating site. This is just one of many ways, Frankie. It is not a perfect science, but what information we do get online is sometimes worth its weight in gold."

"Okay, that was one. Perhaps you just got lucky. How many more could there be?" I asked, still confused over the whole issue.

"It is much more information intense than even the agency can estimate right now. So far we have infiltrated organized crime families, drug cartels, prostitution rings, biker activity, the list goes on and on," Thomas explained.

"Okay, but who is going to use their real identities? No one is going to provide you with detailed information about themselves, online or otherwise are they?" I countered.

"No, but there are many other avenues to look at. Even if real names are not used, accurate locations usually are. Don't forget the people we target are not the top of the hierarchy. They are not the frontrunners in these organizations. They are the superfluous members who think they can fly underneath the radar. We obtain most of our information from the subordinates, not the leaders. And, sometimes," Thomas ventured cautiously. "We can target their family members who may not be completely privy to their activities, but still have contact with them."

And there it was. All the cards were now laid out on the table. I turned around to face him.

"So, first you performed your regular surveillance on me hoping to find Józef. Then, you found out I had signed up on a dating site and you probably all yelled, *Bingo!*"

"I hate to say it, but in your case, it was fairly easy, yes. We usually have to work a lot harder at infiltration. As I said, it is not a perfect science, but any additional avenues we can use help us immensely. NICO can be used with any data base, but the dating sites turned out to be of greater value to us than any of the others."

I watched Thomas take another sip of his water. I could not stand the cottony feel in my mouth any longer. I turned to Józef and said, "Can I please have some water as well?"

He glared at me before yelling, "Marta!"

I had the distinct impression he felt somehow appalled by having to serve me. We waited for no more than a minute or two before Marta walked into the room.

"Prepare some lunch and bring Francesca some water," he barked.

"Sí Señor," she said, and left the room almost bowing.

So she did understand English, I thought. She was just probably too frightened to communicate with me earlier. I shuddered to think about the fear Józef had installed in her as well.

I walked back over to my seat and motioned for Thomas to continue.

"The second half of the *how* pertains to the dating sites themselves, specifically the Canadian ones," he said. "They turned out to be the perfect way in, without raising any red flags."

"But you are with EU Intelligence, not CSIS. Surely Canadian corporations wouldn't just open up their doors to you like that," I countered. "Those companies would never have allowed you to just meander through their data bases and into people's personal lives like that. There are personal security laws they would have to honour."

"Not if we found the perfect backdoor."

CHAPTER 48

Marta's entrance into the room drew my eyes away from Thomas. She served Józef, then handed me a small china plate with a dry-looking sandwich on it and placed a glass of water on the floor beside me.

"Thank you," I said.

Once Marta finished handing Thomas his plate, she left the room and I turned to look at Thomas. "Was this what you were going to tell me in the Lincoln?"

"Yes, I wanted you to know everything."

"Gee, Thomas, that was very considerate of you. Perhaps you might have thought about that days ago," I said, waving my arm around to amplify where we were.

Again, Józef laughed. He was enjoying every moment of this. He loved to see other people unhappy and miserable. Somehow he fed on it.

"Well go on," I said, looking down at my seemingly unpalatable sandwich. "Tell me about this perfect backdoor and what it specifically has to do with Canada."

"Have you heard of Directive 95/46/EC or PIPEDA?" Thomas asked.

"I don't know what Directive 95 whatever is," I said. "But I know PIPEDA is personal security legislation."

"Please allow me to elaborate," Thomas said, pushing himself up trying to get comfortable again. "Directive 95/46/EC addresses the protection of online personal data within the EU. PIPEDA is Canada's rendition of that. The acronym stands for the Personal Information Protection and Electronic Documents Act. It was passed in 1990 and was intended to encourage electronic commerce between the EU and Canada. The EU was reluctant to do business with any country that did not have proper privacy laws in place, so

PIPEDA was Canada's initiative to show the EU their laws were up to par. Within the EU Directive, it was hard to find a loophole, but we discovered one in PIPEDA. In its legislation, section 7 to be exact, it addresses the issue of disclosure without knowledge or consent. It states that organizations may disclose personal information without the knowledge or consent of an individual if the information is related to national security, the defence of Canada or the conduct of international affairs. Basically, we were able to gain access through a number of dating sites, all in the name of national security. The legislation is quite clear, so even if they did run it past a whole slew of their corporate lawyers, ultimately they knew there would be no legal backlash. It is all quite legal, and they knew it."

"Didn't they expect Canadian authorities to be involved?" I asked. "I mean, why would they just turn over their whole system to EU Intelligence?"

"For two reasons," Thomas explained. "One, Canada is a member state of Interpol, an agency that EU Intelligence presides over. And, two, we simply pointed out to these companies they had a responsibility to global security because they recruited clientele from all over the world. Some feared legal repercussions for *not* cooperating, but most were quite accommodating. In a world of incessant terrorist attacks, people like to be part of the solution. It makes them feel good."

"Well, you must all be very proud of yourselves," I said, placing my empty plate on the floor.

"Proud? No," Thomas stated. "Effective? Yes."

I saw Thomas wince again as he tried to reposition himself. I could tell he was in great pain. I guess on some level I still had sympathy for him, despite our current situation. His eyes caught mine and I felt, for a moment, that he knew what I was thinking again.

"There is one thing I still don't understand, Thomas. Why are we all here? What does this have to do with him?" I asked, nodding in Józef's direction.

It was Józef's turn to speak. "The agency does not like someone of my social magnitude knowing such a system exists."

"That is why they have been trying to find you?" I said, withdrawing my attention away from Thomas for a moment.

"It is," Józef said smugly. "There is a terrible lack in security at the agency."

"How did he find out, exactly?" I asked, Thomas.

"Bruyere. We don't know exactly how he found out about NICO, but we think there is a leak within the agency. But this is not important now," Thomas said.

Then Józef began to cackle, and I couldn't stand to look at him anymore, so I returned to my place in front of the window.

Thomas just ignored him. "Frankie, do you have any idea the absolute enormity of this delicate issue? If this information was leaked to the general public, it would not just be people who were affected; entire global economic structures would be destroyed. The security of the Internet world would collapse. Everyone would pull out. It would be cataclysmic. The agency wishes to maintain the utmost secrecy in this matter."

"Don't you mean the agency just wishes to cover their own asses in this matter?" I said.

Thomas ignored my comment as well.

"Your boyfriend here is associated with one nasty agency," Józef said.

It was my turn to do the ignoring.

"I don't understand something. You were supposed to be tracking Józef because Interpol lost him. How is it you already know him?"

"I was not completely honest with you."

I began to pace. This whole scenario was so totally incomprehensible to me. Thomas gave me a moment before continuing.

"Józef and I met at Interpol a while ago," he said. "It was when he was providing information to them. We offered him a better deal and brought him into Intelligence protection. I did not want to tell you I knew him for fear of frightening you off. If you knew I had met your father, you never would have trusted me."

"As opposed to now?" I said sarcastically.

"Touché," Thomas said.

"He went underground, again, after he discovered NICO. This was the true nature of my quest to locate him," he said. "It was imperative I locate him, surely you can now see the potentially disastrous effects here."

CHAPTER 49

I turned around to face Thomas and noticed that Józef had left the room. Apparently there were no more mental blows to inflict on me at the moment, so he must have lost interest. I couldn't believe I did not even hear him leave the room. I was usually quite aware of Józef's movements, especially within such close proximity to me.

I was feeling a bit better after putting something in my stomach, *something* being the operative word, but I was still feeling nauseous. I was glad Józef was no longer in the room. I wanted to talk to Thomas on my own. I walked over to where he was on the sofa. His face was still quite pallid, and he looked like he could sleep for a week, but at least he was alive.

"How are you feeling?" I asked, sincerely.

"I will be fine," he said.

"This is a mess, Thomas."

"I have been feeling quite guilty."

"When did it change?" It was all I said. Thomas knew exactly what I meant.

"Primarily, on the first day," he said. "I am a very good judge of character. You confirmed any lingering suspicions I had on the second day when I realized you never knew Bruyere."

"How did you get into bug my house?" I asked.

"The cleaning crew."

I was passed the point of being surprised anymore. Thomas and I might as well have been having a conversation about the weather for the lack of shock I was showing.

"This NICO program," I began. "You were able to use it to see what I was doing online?"

"Yes."

"So you knew what criteria I typed in that day?"

"Yes. We were able to simultaneously type in the same ones."

"Hence, I would be the one to contact you."

"That is what we were hoping for, yes," Thomas said.

"And the photos?" I asked.

"As an Intelligence agent, I could not use photos of myself. It would be too dangerous. I used ones of my dead brother. The commonalities were just enough to make them seem legitimate."

"And he would have approved of this?" I asked.

"Yes, he would have. He was an agent too."

Józef hobbled back into the room and sat down on his chair.

"Okay," he said. "It is time to figure out a plan of action. I wish I did not need you, Thomas, but unfortunately I do. You know the internal workings of your agency. What will their next move be?"

"First, was that your men who shot at us from outside of Cancun?" Thomas asked.

Józef looked puzzled.

"No," he replied. "I need you alive. You are the one who is going to get me out of this mess. Someone shot at you?"

"Yes, and now you have just confirmed the agency has indeed hired external hit men and have officially removed themselves from the equation, for the time being."

"How did you track us down?" Thomas asked. "I mean to Mexico."

"We have been tracking you since Hythe," Józef said confidently. "Did you not think once my men reported back to me with photos of Bruyere and the young woman he was watching on the beach I would not have recognized my own daughter?"

I looked at Thomas. He avoided eye contact with me. He knew what I was thinking.

"I am going to need access to a mobile phone. Can you get me one?" Thomas asked Józef.

"You can have a disposable one. What else do you need?" he replied, impatiently.

"Some sleep."

"Very well," Józef said, standing up again. "It is too late to do anything today anyway. I will have Marta check on your injuries. I do not want you dying before you can solve this problem for me."

Before he left the room, Józef turned around to look at me, shook his head, laughed to himself and limped away.

"What was that about?" Thomas asked me.

"Nothing," I said, walking over to Thomas. "That was just his way of letting me know how insignificant he thinks I am. Trust me; it's not a new revelation."

Thomas stared at me as I sat down at the end of the sofa, moving his feet slightly out of my way.

I looked at him. "What?"

"I cannot imagine having him as a father."

"Consider yourself lucky," I said, as I leaned back and rested my neck against the top of the sofa.

"Here," Thomas said.

I opened my eyes and looked over towards him, yawning.

"Come and lie down with me. There is enough room."

"Marta will be back to look at you soon. I'll lie down after she has checked you over."

CHAPTER 50

I woke up to the sound of a revving engine outside the window. I sat up and realized I was still at the end of the sofa in the exact same position as I last remembered. I stood up and walked over to the window, straining my eyes to see who it was. I watched as the Cherokee skidded out of the dirt driveway and onto the main road.

"Probably gone to get the mobile phone," Thomas said, behind me.

I turned and walked back to where he was. He looked much better this morning. The colour was back in his face and he was smiling.

"How can you be so cheerful?" I asked, as I sat back down at the end of the filthy sofa.

"You have stopped loathing me, yes?"

"Yes, but just a little," I said, suppressing a grin.

"Where is Józef?"

"I have no idea. Why?" I asked.

"I do not know how openly we can talk right now. He may have this room tapped for all I know. We are going to have to be very careful."

"Do you have a plan?"

Thomas was speaking very quietly now. "In theory, yes, or at least I know what needs to be done. I am still trying to work out the finer points."

"Are you sure you are up to it?" I whispered. "You still need to recuperate."

"I am better than I seem. As for right now, it is better for Józef to think I am in worse shape than I really am."

"Who are you going to call? Your connection in the agency?"

"Actually, Józef is."

"Józef is going to do what?" Józef bellowed, as he entered the room.

"What the hell are you, a bat?" Thomas said sarcastically. "I said you are going to call the agency."

"And why would I do that?" he asked.

"Because you are going to cut a deal with them to bring me in."

"It will never work. They will just kill me, then you," he said, matter-of-factly, then hobbled further into the room.

"Not if you had proof of NICO," Thomas explained. "Besides, they want me much more than they want you. You are nothing to them, a petty stool pigeon who has extricated himself from everyone. You are just a thorn to them. I am the whole bush," Thomas said nonchalantly, looking over at me.

I knew what he was doing, and I was taking great pleasure in watching the ever-evolving shades of red flush over Józef's face.

"You think this inconsequential baiting is going to bother me?" he asked, taking his usual seat.

Thomas smiled. "The colour of your face betrays you, Józef."

Józef slammed his cane down on the ground, then lifted it and pointed it at Thomas. "Listen you little governmental parasite. Talk to me like that again and I will….let's just say it will make Bruyere's unfortunate accident seem like child's play."

"I am sorry to disappoint you, Józef, but you do not intimidate me. Besides, I understand that tongue is an acquired taste, and I am more of a pasta enthusiast."

Józef was fuming, but trying to control it the best he could. I am sure he was not used to people speaking down to him. It must have been a very hard pill to swallow. He stood up glaring at Thomas, then picked up his chair and whipped it straight across the room at me, catching me across both legs. I screamed in pain as the rough metal edge gouged into my right shin. Thomas bolted upright, but as he tried to stand up, he lost his balance and fell back to the sofa. "You bastard," he seethed.

"And do not forget it," Józef snarled and walked out of the room.

"Frankie, come here," Thomas said anxiously.

I was sitting on the floor, looking at the gash in my leg. I stood up when Thomas called me and limped over to where he was on the sofa favouring my right leg.

"Are you all right?"

"I'm fine," I said softly.

Thomas noticed my hands were shaky. "What has he done to you?"

I knew Thomas wasn't talking about my leg anymore. I didn't answer him though. I did not want to relive all the horrible memories of my past again, and by the look on Thomas's face, I didn't think I had to.

He looked at my leg and when he was satisfied it wasn't a serious injury, he took me by my hand and pulled me close to him. He hugged me and whispered into my ear, "It is all going to be fine. Trust me, Bella."

CHAPTER 51

The Cherokee pulled up about an hour later and the two brainless wonders ambled through the front door and down the hallway to where I presumed Józef was waiting. Thomas and I heard the three of them talking somewhere near the rear of the house, but it was too unintelligible to make out what they were saying. We sat there waiting for Józef to emerge.

"Do you think he will follow the plan?" I asked. "You kind of ticked him off."

"I may have temporarily ruffled a few feathers, but Józef will not succumb to my obvious antics. When it comes to business, he will do what is in the best interest of him. I hold a good number of cards right now and he knows this."

"Why antagonize him then?"

"That was purely for you," he said, winking at me.

Both of us cranked our heads towards the hallway as Józef made his entrance into the sitting room, his two lackeys behind him.

"The organ grinder returns," Thomas said, smirking. Then he tilted his head to catch the eyes of the two men behind Józef and said, "Where are your tin cups?"

They both looked at each other, then at Józef. I dared not to laugh, but in my head I was on the floor in stitches.

Józef turned to look at me.

"How is your leg?" he asked.

It was his not-so-subtle retort to Thomas's verbal punches. He was trying to show us exactly who was in charge.

"It will heal quite nicely, thanks. Besides, I don't think you will be able to notice it amongst all the others."

Józef glared at me for a moment trying to figure out if he was just slighted by me or not. He must have deemed it trivial as he opted to turn his head to speak to Thomas instead of pursuing our conversation.

"Here is the cell phone you requested," he said, tossing it to Thomas. "Have you given any thought to an alternative plan, or am I going to have to come up with one?"

"It was not mockery," Thomas said decisively. "I indeed have proof that NICO exists."

"Show me," Józef replied.

"That I cannot do, Józef. I, we, are your prisoners, remember?"

"Tell me then."

Just as Thomas began to speak, Marta entered the room carrying a tray piled with toast and a coffee press filled with what smelled to me like roast chicory. She offered the tray to Józef before serving the rest of us. It was a dominance thing and she obviously knew the pecking order. We each took the cup of coffee Marta offered us, and a wedge of toast from the tray, before Thomas began his sentence again.

"I have the programming language, along with several encrypted internal e-mails that can directly implicate three top officials within the agency and two governmental officials outside of it."

"If they are encrypted, how do you know you have the correct evidence?" Józef asked.

"Because I also have the original cryptovariable to the ciphertext."

"What the hell does that mean?" Józef shouted, quickly losing his patience.

"It means I have the key that can decrypt them back into plain text."

"And you wish for me to call and tell them this?" Józef asked. "And that evidence will convince them?"

Thomas did not answer him right away. We were both now staring at Józef as be began to sway back and forth in his chair. One of his men noticed as well and ran to his side.

"Get away from me you fool," Józef said, striking at him in a feeble attempt, as he gripped his cane to steady himself.

Thomas and I watched as Józef struggled to gain his composure. He looked directly at us and screamed, "You did this!" Then he plummeted to the floor. I stood up in shock, looking back at Thomas, but he had already sprung to his feet and was adjacent to the two men towering over Józef before he was barely in mid collapse. The confusion of Józef's collapse caught the two men off guard and Thomas was able to send one of them sailing across the room with a solid blow to the left side of the head. The taller man retaliated quickly and leapt toward Thomas. I ran to them, grabbing one of the metal chairs in the process and swung for China as it came crashing down on the taller man's head. At first I didn't think I did any damage because he lunged for me, but the second blow that came from Thomas did incapacitate him. He now lay three feet from Józef who was mumbling and writhing on the floor, as drool seeped out of the corner of his mouth. Then, without warning, the first man Thomas had struck was now coming back at us. As he dove for Thomas's body, the two of them went soaring across the other side of the room in a flurry of arms and legs. I cringed as I heard their collective weight hit the floor. I looked around for Marta, knowing she would have surely heard the entire ruckus by now and could perhaps be calling for more of Józef's men to arrive, but she was nowhere to be seen. She was probably too scared to do anything at all, I thought. At least at the moment, I hoped she was. Before I realized what was happening with the tangle of bodies on the floor, Thomas emerged on top and was diligently laying blows to the man's face rendering him unconscious as well.

He stood up, weaving slightly and panting, "Grab the mobile phone while I tie Józef up."

I ran to the phone and jammed it deep inside my pocket. I turned towards the front door and stopped to look at Józef lying on the floor. He was laying in a crumpled mess of lost decorum.

"How?" I asked, now looking towards Thomas, but he was diligently working at tying up Józef's limbs and did not answer me.

When he was done, and satisfied he had secured him well enough, Thomas quickly dragged the other two men one by one into the bathroom by the front door and wedged a chair up against the outside of the door handle hindering their escape.

"It is not ideal, but it should hold them," Thomas said, grabbing my hand and heading towards the front door. "Quickly."

I pulled back on Thomas's hand for a moment. He stopped in mid step and looked back at me in confusion. I let go of his hand and walked back over to where Józef was on the floor. He was still slightly conscious, but to what extent I did not know. He did not seem to have the capability to look up at me, and I was totally clueless as to whether he could understand me or not. I stood there for several moments staring down at him. He was finally weaker than I was. I could almost do anything to him right now and there would be nothing he could do in retaliation, I thought. Unlike him, though, I did not feel power or control. I felt only indignity and disgrace that the pathetic lump on the floor was biologically related to me.

I slowly turned around as Thomas touched my shoulder.

"Frankie, we must leave now."

I turned to walk away. Just as Thomas and I were closing the front door, I could have sworn I heard Józef mumble, 'Bitch,' but I couldn't be sure.

We hopped into the red Cherokee and Thomas turned the ignition. It was not surprising to find the keys already in the truck. We were in the middle of nowhere. I couldn't imagine Józef being too pleased with his two henchmen's lack of attention to detail, but then again they weren't exactly protégés of Einstein.

As Thomas pulled out of the driveway, he asked for the mobile phone. I handed it to him then looked back towards the house. In the top window, I saw Marta standing there holding back a curtain.

"Thomas!" I yelled, "Marta is watching us!"

"Calm down. It is fine. She is just waiting for us to leave so she can make her long journey back to her family in Puebla. She has the keys to another car parked at the back of the house."

I stared at Thomas for a moment. "It was her!"

"Yes," Thomas said.

"How? When? Why?" I stammered.

Thomas simply grinned, pointed a finger towards himself and said, "Charming, remember?"

I laughed, and feigned a smack to his arm.

"How did she do it?"

"Rohypnol."

"The date rape drug?" I asked, shocked.

"Has a solid affect though. It works very quickly and typically lasts for four to six hours."

"Where did she get it?"

"She is a trained medical professional, remember?"

I nodded.

Thomas picked up the cell phone and dialled a number as I watched the road ahead of us and behind us. I had now become an incessant observer of my surroundings.

"It is me," Thomas said, into the phone.

I listened and tried to make sense out of the one-sided conversation I was overhearing.

"In Mexico...I am not sure...Yes, it was him...Of course...Where?...And the gunmen?...Fine...Yes, I will do that."

Thomas ended the call and pulled over to the side of the road. He used the keys to pry open the back of the cell phone. A smile crept across his face as he peered inside. He opened up his door, walked to the other side of the road and placed the cell phone in the grass beside it. Then he walked back to the truck and got in. As he pulled back onto the road, he looked at me and said, "Józef is not so clever after all. He should never have assumed all disposable mobile phones came without GPS chips."

"I don't understand," I said, to Thomas. "Why would you call the agency? That will bring them, and the gunmen, even closer to us."

"That was not the agency, Frankie."

"Then who was it?" I asked, even more confused now.

"It was the Polish mafia."

CHAPTER 52

I sat staring at Thomas as we drove onto yet another highway. "You have the phone number to someone in the Polish mafia confined to memory?"

"Not exactly. That was an associate of mine. The actual phone call will go through him."

"So now Józef is a dead man?"

"He always was," Thomas said, veering the truck to the left. "It was only a matter of time. All I did was speed up the process. I now know you will be safe, at least from him."

I wasn't exactly surprised by Thomas's phone call. Sadly, I was becoming quite desensitized to his world now. I think what bothered me the most is the fact that somehow I felt like I had a hand in it. I did not want to be responsible for Józef's death, even if I was only guilty by association.

"That doesn't sit too well with me, Thomas."

"I know, but it had to be done."

"Couldn't you just have let it all run its natural course?"

Thomas was quiet for a moment before answering me. Usually when he did that, he was contemplating how to say something to me. I was getting quite used to his character traits.

"Spit it out, Thomas."

"He was going to kill you, along with me."

I sat silently, then turned to look out the window.

"How?" I asked.

"The particulars are not important. Please do not torture yourself with this. You are not his daughter in his eyes. He sees the world in a totally different perspective than you and I. We were purely an article of leverage to him. Nothing more."

"Marta told you?"

"Yes, she did. She overheard a lot of things."

"Will she be all right?" I asked.

"I believe so."

Thomas turned the Cherokee off the highway and into a small town. I did not see the name of it. It was either too small to warrant a highway sign, or I was too engrossed in our conversation about how my own father was going to kill me to notice it.

"How do you know where we are?" I asked Thomas.

"There is only one highway, Frankie. Sooner or later it would have either led us to a town I recognized or led us to one where we could get some directions from. As for right now, I am more concerned at obtaining amenities. We need food, shelter, a long hot shower and about twelve solid hours of uninterrupted kip."

"Look at us, Thomas. People will ask questions."

"This is Mexico. People are more apt to mind their own business. Down here, asking questions can get you killed."

Within twenty minutes, Thomas and I were walking into our room at the Mira Flores hotel in a sleepy little town I could not pronounce the name of.

CHAPTER 53

The next morning, I awoke to the sound of a tractor tending its acreage. For a brief second, I dreamt of lawn mowers and my house in Dundas, but reality set in very quickly as I rolled over and felt the sharp pain of a still-open wound on my right shin. I heard the shower running and glanced around the room. Thomas must have been up with the sun, I thought. There was fresh fruit and coffee waiting for me on a tray at the end of the bed. I glanced over at the clock. It was 6:53 a.m.

I reached down towards the end of the bed and lifted two juicy slices of pineapple off the plate and settled back against the headboard. I heard the shower turn off and a few moments later, Thomas emerged.

His body was bruised from head to toe.

"You look like something the cat dragged in," I said.

"I feel like something the cat dragged in," he replied, taking a piece of mango from the same plate.

"How did you pay for all of this?"

"Józef kidnapped us, Bella. He did not rob us."

"Ah, so where do we go from here?" I asked, scooting down to the end of the bed again to pinch another piece of fruit. I chose two plump strawberries this time.

"It is time to take control of the situation again," he said, as he began to get dressed. "There are still at least two hit men out there that need to be eradicated."

"How?" I asked, as I too started to get dressed.

"We need to get to Tulúm."

Thomas went to pick up a few items from the hotel's meagre supply of amenities, as I made my way towards the truck. He emerged a few moments later gripping a couple of bottles of water and two packets of corn nuts.

"Did you get directions for the quickest route there?" I asked.

"I don't need directions, Bella, I will only ever ask for instructions," Thomas said, with a smug grin.

"What's the difference?" I asked, laughing.

"Directions are usually geographic. Instructions achieve a much better end result."

"Such as?"

"Instructions are more like, a little to the left or a bit more to the right."

Thomas and I laughed again, and it felt good. The two of us had been to hell and back over the last week, and we truly needed some normality back in our lives. I felt a bit guilty laughing and carrying on when I knew what Józef's fate was, perhaps even as we spoke.

"Do you think Józef is still alive?" I asked.

"Why do you wish to burden your mind with such thoughts? I truly wish you would alleviate yourself from such responsibility. It has nothing to do with you. You should let it go."

I knew Thomas was right. Józef chose his life; I did not choose it for him. Whatever happens to him now has nothing to do with me, I thought. It was hard not to think about what they would do to him though. I could not imagine the atrocities, and yet my mind was doing a very good job at providing me with quite a few vivid images.

"We are only about a half hour outside of Tulúm," Thomas said, interrupting my thought process, something I was very thankful for.

"I can assume we are still heading to the safe house?"

"Yes, as I said, I can accomplish much more there. They not only have the security we require, but also the equipment."

"Equipment?"

"Nothing special," Thomas explained. "Basically, just a computer with Internet access and a mobile phone is all I require, but not having to look over our shoulders all the time and having access to clean clothes and a shower has a nice ring to it as well."

"Yes, it does," I said. "But will it house women's clothes in a size 7?"

We drove into Tulúm with our eyes wide open, especially when driving through intersections. Realistically, we knew Józef's men would not give us anymore trouble, but the remnants of what we had just been through were still quite fresh in our minds.

Thomas drove through the main street, *Avenida Tulúm*, turned right onto a side road, then drove to the end of that road and pulled up in front of a large iron gate, decorated with security cameras. Thomas picked up the security phone he could reach from the confines of the Cherokee and announced our arrival. A moment later the gate creaked open and allowed us to enter the premises.

As Thomas drove to the front of the house, which was quite large in stature, I took in my surroundings. Off to my right, I observed two security guards walking at the periphery of the grounds carrying at least one semi-automatic weapon each. To my left, I noticed more security cameras and a guard house, and in front of me, on the second-level mezzanine, I saw two more guards who were intensely watching our vehicle. They also carried Uzis, but unlike the other men, their weapons weren't slung over their shoulders. They were pointed directly at us.

"Do not let them intimidate you, Frankie. We are quite safe here," Thomas said reassuringly, as he stopped the truck and shut down the engine.

"What is this place?" I asked, following Thomas out of the vehicle.

The front door opened and a man wearing khaki trousers and a white t-shirt came out to greet us, with a big smile on his face. Thomas immediately went to him, extending his hand in greeting. They shook hands and gave each other a hug. I wasn't sure if Thomas was just anxious to see him, or happy for the immediate interruption as to avoid answering my question. I thought perhaps it was the latter and quickly decided it was probably better for me not to know where we were or who owned the house.

"Alejandro, esta es Frankie. Habla ingles por favour," Thomas said.

"Of course," the man said, walking towards me. "Hello, Frankie. Welcome to my villa."

"It is very nice to meet you, Alejandro," I said. "Thank you for your hospitality."

"You are welcome," Alejandro said, to me. Then he turned to Thomas and said, "She is quite exquisite, Thomas. I can see why you wanted to go to such great lengths to protect her."

Alejandro escorted Thomas and me through the front doors as two servants approached us with two snifters filled with a golden amber liquid. Whiskey? I thought. Thomas and I each took one of the warm snifters, and I tipped it towards my lips. It was Brandy. The hot liquid eased down my parched throat, slightly stinging it in the process, but it was most welcome nonetheless. Thomas requested I go with the female servant up the stairs and allow her to take care of me. I think the look on my face gave away my fear.

"It is fine. I will be up straight away. I just need to speak with Alejandro for a moment or two. Trust me, please."

I did what Thomas asked and followed the woman up the elaborately carpeted spiral staircase, downing the rest of my brandy in the process. At the top of the stairs, I looked back towards Thomas, but he was already out of sight. The woman motioned for me to follow her into the first room on the right. She did not seem to speak English, so instead of trying to communicate with her through my weak knowledge of the Spanish language, I just followed her lead and allowed her to fuss over me. She walked into the bathroom and proceeded to run a bath for me. Then she walked back into the bedroom and assisted me with my clothing. As I undressed, she took each item from me and desperately tried to hide her aversion to the smell, but I knew what she was thinking. As I held out the next item of clothing to her, I plugged my nose and started to laugh. She laughed as well. There was no lack of communication here. I guess the gesture pretty much translated the same in every language.

As I stood in my bra and panties, the woman took a plush white housecoat off the end of the bed and held it out for me. I took it from her graciously as she nudged me towards the bathroom door. I walked across the room and into the black and white tiled bathroom, dropping the rest of my clothing on the royal blue rug in front of the mirrors, and stepped into the claw foot bathtub. The soapy water immediately stung my leg, but I didn't care. It felt wonderful.

After my body adjusted to the water temperature, I lay back and allowed the hot water to caress my muscles and ease my pains. This time the bubble bath smelled of lilac.

I almost fell asleep, but then I heard the bedroom door open and it startled me.

"It is only me."

I immediately let my shoulders drop and tried to regain my relaxed posture. I wondered if I was ever going to stop being so jumpy.

"In here, Thomas," I said.

Thomas walked into the bathroom, his arms full of shampoo and towels.

"Mind if I join you?" he asked, placing the toiletries and towels on the counter.

"Not at all," I replied, dipping down further into the water. "I love the old claw foot tubs. There is just so much room to lose yourself in."

I watched Thomas struggle with removing his clothing. The left side of his body was almost completely bruised from stem to stern. There were several cuts on his back and what looked like a burn mark across his left thigh. Then I remembered one of Józef's men dragging him across the gravel. It was probably road rash, I thought.

"Been in a fight with a komodo dragon lately?" I asked, jokingly.

"Nope. Tree gecko, but he was tough."

"I am sure he was," I said, laughing.

"You should see him though," Thomas said, laughing. "Oh, and just for the record, I won."

"Of course," I said, splashing water at him as he stepped into the bathtub with me. "No ego there, huh, Thomas?"

"Of course," he said, smiling.

"That's not an answer," I said, laughing. "That's an evasion."

Thomas was having the same difficulties edging himself into the soapy water that I did.

"Stings a bit, doesn't it?"

"I can take it," he said, smiling and intentionally lowering his voice.

I splashed more water at him and waited for him to settle at the opposite end of the bathtub.

"It's quite nice once the stinging subsides, isn't it?" I said.

His reply was a very relaxing sigh. I watched him as he closed his eyes and rested his head against the wall tiles. I stared at him for a moment wondering how I could have gotten through this without him. I came to the conclusion quite sometime ago that regardless of whether Thomas was the one to track me down or not, eventually the agency would have come for me anyway. It was truly a blessing that Thomas was the lead agent on this assignment.

"If it wasn't for you, I'd be dead right now," I simply stated.

Thomas slowly opened his eyes, lifted his head up, and looked at me.

"Perhaps," he said. "Perhaps not."

"No it's true. I genuinely believe that, and I just wanted to say thank you. I know it sounds lame, but I wanted to say it anyway."

Thomas looked at me before replying. Then he said, "Perhaps it is actually you who has saved me. Now come here."

CHAPTER 54

After Thomas and I emerged from our, umm, two-hour-long bath, which left the whole of the bathroom in a soaking mess, we wrapped ourselves up in our housecoats and walked into our bedroom to find fresh clothes awaiting us.

"I never heard anyone come into the room," I said, a bit surprised.

"I do believe you were preoccupied," he said, laughing.

"You mean..."

Thomas laughed again. "Your face is flushed," he said, pointing at me.

"It is not," I said defensively. "I just got out of a hot bathroom."

Then he laughed again.

The Armani jeans were just slightly big on me, but the pale pink angora sweater fit brilliantly. I didn't want to put on my old bra and panties, so I decided to go commando instead – a decision Thomas found very appealing.

Thomas looked very striking in his new attire. He wore a pair of Versace black pants and a pale grey Moschino sweater, with three buttons at the neckline. Then he produced some Hugo Boss cologne from the other side of the room and dabbed some on his neck.

"How did you come to be so spoiled?" I asked.

"If you are feeling left out, you will find some Samsara on the table behind you."

"How did they..." I began, but then I remembered Thomas had already planned for us to be here, before Józef interjected.

"Thank you."

"My pleasure, now come with me. I want to go downstairs to have a bite to eat."

We sat down to a lovely table that was covered with a red and white checkered table cloth and garnished with all sorts of breads and meats and cheeses. Thomas poured us each a glass of wine, and we began to feast.

"This tastes magnificent," I mumbled, my mouth filled with brie cheese and black olives.

Thomas nodded as he stuffed another pita triangle into his mouth.

"Thomas, can I ask you something?"

"Of course."

"There are a lot of things that have become clear to me over the last week or so, but the one thing I still don't understand is your e-mail from Lebanon."

"I am not sure I understand, Bella."

"Okay, you pretended to be a volunteer doctor, because it would impress me, I can understand that. You pretended to e-mail me from a war-torn country, something I could relate to, and I can understand that. But why was it written so graphically? I mean, you used such detail and sentiment, it made it so real. I guess I just don't understand how someone can be that emotional about someplace they never were. How could you just lie like that, and in such detail? To be quite honest, it scares me a bit."

"And why do you think I was never there?" Thomas asked, placing some jalapeño havarti cheese onto another wedge of pita bread.

"Because it was all part of the set up to attract me to you, wasn't it?"

"Yes and no. Our e-mails were part of my assignment, but you were quite easy to chat with. I felt comfortable with you. In another life time, I was a doctor. And, yes, I had been in Lebanon. Perhaps not at the time I was e-mailing you, but I did draw from a past experience there. It was not all a lie, Frankie."

"I am not sure what to say, Thomas. I am sorry."

"You have nothing to apologize for. I am very happy with the way things have turned out. I became involved with the agency because of my brother, but that is a story for another time. Right now, I have to set some wheels in motion."

"It's all become one big butterfly effect, hasn't it?"

"Yes, it has," Thomas said, as he pushed his chair out from the table and wiped his mouth on a linen napkin.

"What would you like me to do?" I asked.

"Nothing," Thomas said, smiling. "I will not be long. I have to make a few phone calls, look up some information on the Internet, and courier a package overseas. Once those items are off the agenda, you and I can start packing."

"Where are we going now?" I asked, feeling a bit startled.

"Relax. I thought perhaps I would come back with you to Dundas for a while."

I sat there stunned. I think my jaw hit the floor.

"How?" It was all I could stammer out.

"I have already told you. I now have the encryption key that links NICO to some very important people."

"I thought it was a bluff!"

"No, it was not. It has been a long haul, but my connection within the agency has proved to be a very lucrative one. He and I have known for quite some time how untenable our futures were with the agency. We planned appropriately. It was all just a matter of him being able to get the evidence out of Belgium and into Tulúm. Perhaps one day you will meet him."

"So we are really going home?"

Thomas laughed. "Yes, we are really going home."

"Can I call Marianne?"

"To be quite honest, I would like to wait until we leave Mexico, but if you really feel it necessary, I will see that you can. Please, just be careful as to what you tell her. She, nor anyone else for that matter, can ever know about NICO."

"I really have to call her Thomas. She is probably going out of her mind."

"I will not be long. I will see you upstairs in a short while."

Thomas walked over to me, gave me a quick peck on the lips, and left the room. I reached over the table and poured myself another glass of wine, then I raised my glass into the air.

"Here's to going home."

CHAPTER 55

As promised, Thomas did not take long to finish what he was doing. He walked back into our room about a half hour later.

"All done," he said, walking towards me and holding out his arms.

I hugged him tightly. I could not believe it was finally all going to be over. "Are you sure this will keep them at bay?" I asked, leaning back to look at his face.

"Yes. Even the hit men have been called off."

"I just can't get over it. I mean I just can't get my head wrapped around the idea of feeling safe again."

"I do not wish to give you the wrong impression. We are relatively safe. That is the best I can do."

"Are they going to allow you to just walk away from the agency like that?"

"At the moment, yes, as long as I am holding all the cards. Unfortunately, I cannot tell you what the future may hold. But let us not think about that at the moment. It could be a very long way off. I think right now we should be making our way to Cancun. Our flight does not leave until tomorrow morning, but I thought it would be nice to spend at least one day in the sun before we left. It is a beautiful place. We could take a nice long leisurely stroll along the white sand beaches, without having to look over our shoulders."

"I think that is a brilliant idea."

The drive along the Cancun-Chetumal 307 highway was wonderfully relaxing. It was only a two-hour drive from Tulúm to Cancun, and Thomas and I weren't in any particular hurry to get there, so we drove at an unhurried pace with our windows rolled down trying to catch intermittent glances at the crystal blue ocean off to our right.

I bent over and squeezed Thomas's hand. "Thanks for setting up the phone call between Marianne and me."

"I take it she was pleased to hear from you?"

"That is an understatement," I said, laughing. "Don't be surprised if she meets us at the airport."

"She sounds like a very good friend."

"It will probably take me a week to explain everything to her."

"Yes, but not before we remove all the transmitters from your house."

"I almost forgot about those."

"Do not worry," he said, squeezing my hand. "I will take care of everything."

Thomas pulled into the parking area of the Hotel Calinda and parked across from the main entrance of the hotel. He went in to register as I waited in the car. I wanted to stay outside as long as I possibly could. I cherished being outdoors now. I watched Thomas exit the hotel and walk over to the truck. I smiled. He was truly the most magnificent man I had ever met. My grandmother used to tell me timing was everything and everything happened for a reason. Perhaps this was the reason I had been single for so long. I was unknowingly waiting for Thomas.

Thomas hopped back into the truck and pulled around to the other side of the hotel. He backed into parking spot 101, shut down the engine and stepped out of the truck, stretching his arms. He walked around to the other side of the truck and waited for me. We walked in silence through the back entrance of the hotel and into the marble-tiled elevator. Our room was only one floor up, but we were still too sore to make the effort to climb the stairs. The elevator stopped and Thomas and I stepped off of it and followed the arrow to

Room 101. Thomas swiped the security lock on the door with our room card and we stepped inside.

"You and I roaming in and out of different hotel rooms is starting to become a habit with us," I said, laughing.

"It could be worse," he said. "Should we go for that walk on the beach now?"

"Later," I said, wrapping my arms around his neck and pushing the door closed with my foot. "Right now I have other plans for you."

CHAPTER 56

I was lying on my side, with Thomas's arm draped over my body feeling the safest I had in what seemed like an eternity, then rolled over to kiss him.

"As much as I am enjoying this, I think I'd like that walk on the beach," I said.

Thomas moaned. I tried to lift his arm off my body, but he was resisting. I laughed. "You are going to have to let me up at some point, Thomas."

"No."

"Yes," I said, still laughing and trying again to lift his arm up.

Then he let go. "All right, you win."

I stood up, put on my clothes, and walked across the room and into the bathroom. I looked around and walked back into the other room where Thomas was now sitting at the edge of the bed.

"We forgot the bags in the truck," I said. "I'll just quickly run down and get them."

Thomas yawned. "No, I will go. I need to go to the front desk anyway."

Thomas pulled on his pants and sweater, then walked over to me and gave me a long drawn-out kiss on the lips.

"This is good," he said.

"Yes, it is."

I knew he meant more than just the kiss. He meant us. It was nice feeling this comfortable with someone, this secure, this safe.

As Thomas made his way out the door, I walked out onto the balcony that overlooked the parking lot. It was a gorgeous day. I couldn't wait to go for that walk on the beach. I looked down when I saw Thomas appear from the corner of my eye. He looked up at me and smiled.

"Can I bring you anything from the lobby?" he asked.

"No thanks, just you," I beamed.

I leaned on the railing as Thomas made his way towards the Cherokee and began to wonder how this whole situation had ever come to be. My grandmother always cited fate as a strong force in our lives, but this was still even a bit too unfathomable even for me. Here I was in love with a man who I met on the Internet, who had lied about his identity, and who was now going to be a big part of my life. What started out as me wanting a few casual dates had now turned into a full-blown romance. My grandmother always used to say, "Frankie, life is what happens while you are making plans." I think it was an old John Lennon quote.

I watched as Thomas walked around to the back of the truck and opened the hatch to get our bags. As the latch popped open, all I felt was the Cherokee's shattered glass flying at me and the immense heat coming from the backlash of the explosion.

CHAPTER 57

I woke up on the balcony floor with a medic bent over me and two hotel clerks standing behind him. I tried to stand up, but they wouldn't let me.

"Where is Thomas?" I demanded. "Let me up!"

The medic didn't really want to let me stand up, but in the end, he had no choice. I fought my way up and looked down at the parking lot, cutting my bare feet on the shards of glass in the process. All I saw was the frame of the blackened Cherokee, a fire truck, a lot of smoke, and a handful of people the police were trying to keep back.

I turned to look at the three men surrounding me. "Where is he?" I yelled.

"Señorita, please calm down," a man said. He appeared to be the hotel manager. "The gentleman in the truck, he is gone. I am sorry."

"Where?" I yelled.

"An ambulance is taking him to the morgue. Again, I am sorry. Is there anyone I can call for you?"

I never answered him. I just stood there staring at the charcoal mess that lay below me. I heard a knock on the door and ran into the room to open it, despite the sharp pains in my feet. "Thomas?" I yelled. But as I opened the door, all I saw on the other side of it was two police officers.

"Señorita, may we please speak with you?"

After sixteen hours of interrogation, an escort to the airport by a Mexican police officer, and a representative from the Canadian consulate in Cancun, I was now sitting on a Boeing 757 on my way back to Canada.

The authorities tried grilling me for information for what seemed like an eternity. I think they suspected Thomas and I were involved in something illegal. But the consulate official said they had to either charge me or let me go within twenty-four hours. So, in the end, knowing they were not getting anywhere questioning me, and they didn't have any evidence to charge me with, they chose the latter and shipped me back to Canada with an emergency passport the consulate expedited for me.

I sat staring out the window expecting to turn around and find Thomas sitting beside me, but I knew it wasn't going to happen. We had come so far together. We had gone through so much, and now it was all gone. Everything that had meant anything was just gone.

I don't really remember the actual flight. I think I was too numb. I remembered boarding the plane in Cancun and feeling like a wanton criminal with dozens of people watching as I was escorted onto the plane. I remembered landing at the Hamilton International Airport and taking a taxi to Dundas, but that was more because it just felt very strange to be home again.

Marianne was already at my house waiting for me when the taxi pulled up in the driveway. The Canadian consulate needed a contact name and number from Canada, and Marianne was the natural choice. They gave her the information regarding my flight and made sure she was waiting here for me upon my arrival, just as she was always there for me no matter what.

I was now sitting in my living room, sipping a cup of Earl Grey out of my favorite Arsenal mug, and looking across the room at the three men scouring through my home. Marianne was sitting on my couch doing her best to console me.

"Thanks for them," I said, nodding towards the detectives.

Marianne had hired three off-duty police detectives to locate and remove any of the transmitters that had been planted in my house. I don't know what she told them, but they didn't ask any questions

"It's nice to have a brother-in-law as a Crown Attorney," she said, smiling.

"Didn't they ask you why my house was bugged?"

"Nope. I think Mathew just told them something about precautions and you being a witness to something. Hey, they're getting paid off-hour wages for this. I don't think they really care too much about the particulars."

"Thanks, Mare. I really appreciate it. I also appreciate the company."

I told her about Józef and the mafia, I told her about what happened to Thomas and what he did for a living, but I never mentioned NICO. I think she knew there was more to the story than I was telling her, but she never pushed me on it. I was very grateful she didn't. It was hard for me to keep things from her, but her security was much more important to me than the few pangs of guilt I felt for not being able to be completely honest with her.

Marianne was quiet for a moment. I knew she wanted to ask me something, but she was having trouble getting to it. Then she finally said, "Are they flying his body back to England?"

I was staring out the glass doors again, something that was becoming a habitual custom of mine now. "I have no idea," I said, sighing. "They wouldn't even let me see him, Mare. Can you believe it? They said I wasn't family and that I was going to have to contact his next of kin if I wanted to see him."

"I suppose you and he never discussed his parents, did you?"

"He said his parents still lived in England, and I know he has family in Mexico, but what they will do with him from here is completely beyond me. I think that is what hurts the most. I will never know where his body was sent to. I could never visit him."

Another tear began to stream down my face. Marianne stood up and walked into the kitchen. When she emerged, she was holding a glass of red wine for me.

"I am going to let you get some rest now, okay? I will see these guys out. You just make sure the door is locked behind me. I will be back in the morning to check on you."

I nodded.

After everyone had gone, I made my way upstairs to my bedroom. I had looked forward to seeing Thomas wake up in the very bed I was about to crawl into, but now I sat down on the end of it feeling cold and alone.

"Why did they have to take you from me, Thomas?" I said, another tear streaking down my face.

The only thing I wasn't so sure about was where Thomas stashed the evidence of NICO. For all I knew, I was still being watched. For all I knew, I could jump into my car tomorrow and it could blow up as well. Somehow, though, I truly didn't think Thomas would have left any holes in the dike when it came to my safety. But it was something he said to me in Mexico that echoed through my head as I finally lay down to sleep. He said, "I do not wish to give you the wrong impression. We are relatively safe. That is the best I can do."

CHAPTER 58

The next morning I woke up in a cold sweat. My whole night was one giant fitful sleep riddled with incoherent nightmares. I must have relived the explosion at least a dozen times and each time I witnessed it, I seemed to be in a different country. At one point, I think I too was blown up. Nevertheless, I was glad the night was finally over.

I sat at the side of my bed for a brief moment wiping my eyes. They felt like sandpaper. I knew a long, hot shower would help, so I tottered off to the bathroom and turned on the taps.

A half hour later I emerged feeling somewhat physically refreshed, if not mentally. That would take time. As I walked through the living room on my way to the kitchen, I felt a slight breeze across my bare feet. I turned around and noticed my sliding glass door was ajar. I walked over and shut it wondering if I had simply forgotten to close it yesterday. I couldn't remember. I was that exhausted. I filled a pot up with water and placed it on the element. I turned to reach for my mug on top of the fridge, but something stopped me dead in my tracks and I dropped my mug. No it couldn't be. Fastened to the door of the fridge was a photo of Marta. Dead. I was sure it was her, and I was sure she was dead. Her head was askew in the most awkward position and she was covered in blood. Her features were unmistakable, though, right down to the baby blue apron she wore when Thomas and I were there. I started to shake. I quickly spun around to survey the room but no one was there. I called out at the top of my lungs, "Who's there?"

But there was no answer. I didn't think there would be. I knew who ever broke into my house and left the photo was probably gone by now. "Why would they stick around?" I reasoned. This is obviously what they intended to leave. If they wanted me, they would have made the effort.

I turned back around and removed the photo from underneath the magnet. What the hell did it mean? I wondered. Was it a threat from the agency? Was this to show me that everyone who could have possibly known about NICO was now dead? Was this their way of telling me I was next?

I turned off the element that was now a vivid shade of red and sat down at the kitchen table to take a proper look at the photo. Poor woman, I thought. Why did they have to kill you? Then another thought occurred to me. What if it wasn't the agency at all? Come to think of it, it wasn't really the agency's style. Their tactics were far more subtle, like blowing up vehicles in broad daylight or shooting at you driving down a highway. They didn't play these kinds of games. What would they gain by this kind of scare tactic?

Then another thought occurred to me. A very unnerving thought. My hand began to shake. This would be exactly the kind of sick and twisted thing Józef would do. But how? No it couldn't be, I reasoned with myself. Józef was dead. Thomas saw to that. But then again there was no proof. We didn't actually witness his death. Could he still be alive? Was our escape way too easy? Was that a set up too? No, it couldn't be. Józef would never have let himself be humiliated like that. He would never have let himself be taken down like that, at least not willingly. Then again, desperation can mean mistakes. I was beginning to feel sick to my stomach again.

The phone rang, and I nearly jumped out of my skin. I stood up to answer it, steadying myself in the process.

"Hello?" I said, my voice sounding a bit unsteady.

There was no one there.

"Hello?" I repeated.

Then I heard it. That unmistakable voice.

"Hello, Francesca."

I froze. My mouth felt like cotton, and I felt myself teetering back and forth from my toes to my heals. I gripped on to the counter for balance.

"Francesca. We have unfinished business."

"What do you want?"

"Meet me at 3:00 p.m. in the parking lot at Spencer Gorge. You know what I want."

"No," I said, wondering where I was finding the strength to stay standing upright. "If we have to meet at all, I want it to be some place very public."

I heard Józef grunt. I knew I was frustrating him. I also knew I was probably pushing him a bit, but I was quickly beginning to realize that maybe I was in more of a position of power than I had previously thought. He still thought I had NICO.

"Actually, Józef, if you want to talk, you can meet me at Limeridge Mall on Upper Wentworth. Buy a map. It's easy to find. It's on the mountain just off the Lincoln Alexander Parkway. I will meet you at the food court on the lower level."

"Fine," he said, through what sounded like gritted teeth.

We hung up, and I stood looking down at the phone for a moment. Then I looked up at the clock. I had exactly six hours and fifteen minutes to figure out a game plan.

CHAPTER 59

By 2:30 p.m. I was pretty much ready to leave for Limeridge Mall, but I was still a bundle of nerves. All afternoon, I kept going over things in my head. Was this a set up? Was the agency involved with Józef again? I knew the agency would never let me out of their sight, at least not as long as they were still searching for the files that would confirm NICO's existence. But first, I had to find them. Then I had to create some foolproof way of protecting them, and myself. But that was another issue. Right now I still had to contend with Józef.

I figured if I could convince Józef I would help him, I would be able to effectively execute my plan to finally escape his clutches. The only problem was, would it work? The way I saw it, I only had one shot at this. After that, Józef would be back in control and, without a doubt, retaliate.

I left my house looking diligently over my shoulder. I could feel the agency's eyes upon me, even if I couldn't physically see them. I wondered if they were even in proximity to me, or if they were simply monitoring me via satellite. I had learned, in a very short period of time, what the agency was capable of doing and what technology they had at their fingertips. I only knew a mere iota of their capabilities, and it scared me to death. The agency held their cards very close to their chest. The general population had no clue. In retrospect, I felt like an idiot. I always assumed our government agencies always had our best interest at hand. I thought it almost impossible for them to hide any threats, new technologies, etc., from the general population because of the diligence of our media. I was exceedingly wrong. Even the existence of the Internet should have opened my eyes a lot earlier than this. The research for the Internet began in the 1950's, but it was the US Air Force who actually commissioned the study that resulted in a network that used packet switching as opposed to circuit switching. The first node went live at UCLA on October 29th 1969 on something called the ARPANET – the mother of the Internet. If there was ever any doubt in my mind that either the elite conspiracy theorists or the independent parliamentary researchers were wrong, I had no doubts now. These truly were the people who had their thumb on the pulse of our governments.

As I drove into the parking lot, I looked for a place to park that was closest to the exit of the mall, just in case I needed an easy escape. I locked my car, walked into the southeast entrance and turned left towards the food court. Along the way, I caught a reflection of myself in one of the glass displays. I looked scared. I was going to have to pull myself together and look much more confident if I was going to pull this off, I told myself.

I turned the corner and walked down the hallway to the food court. I felt like Sean Penn in, *Dead Man Walking*. As I passed Tim Horton's coffee house, I spotted Józef sitting with a woman next to a fake tree just off to the right of the main seating area. I looked around. The place was fairly busy, so I felt a bit safer.

I sat down across from Józef and stared directly at the woman. She smiled, but not affectionately. I looked at Józef.

"You look worried, Francesca."

"I don't trust you. What is it you wanted to discuss?" I asked, looking over at the woman again. Apparently, no one was going to introduce us.

"First let me congratulate you on your endeavours in Mexico. You and your boyfriend certainly caught me off guard, which is not easily done. Kudos," he offered. "Had it not been for that stupid bitch I hired, you never would have succeeded."

Then a slight grin crept across his mouth.

"By the way, you have my condolences."

Józef left his last sentence hanging in mid air. I whipped my head around and glared at him. He knew! How did he know?

"You bastard," I seethed. "It was you!"

"You should never have gotten involved with him."

I jumped up from the table and lunged at Józef. He was still surprisingly strong, despite his meagre frame. He grabbed on to my wrists and forced me back into my seat. A few people at the surrounding tables looked over, but then they just tried to ignore what they saw. In their eyes, Józef was probably too old to be perceived as a threat. They probably thought I was the instigator. It's funny how women could get away with a lot more when it came to violence.

"Sit down, Francesca. You're making a fool out of yourself."

I sat back fuming.

"I hate you." It was all I could say.

"Well, I hate to burst your bubble, daughter, but it wasn't me. I never killed him."

I stared at Józef for what seemed like an eternity, but for some reason, I knew he was telling the truth. I don't know if it was the expression on his face, or the fact I knew he would take great pleasure in telling me if he did do it, but either way he really had nothing to gain by denying it.

"Who then?" I asked.

He shrugged and took a sip of his coffee.

"I would presume the agency," he offered.

"And Marta?" I asked.

"Her blood is on your hands, Francesca, not mine. You should never have involved her."

"You truly are an uncaring bastard, aren't you?"

"Yes, I know," Józef said, shrugging. "Can we get back to business now, or would you like to take another leap at me? By the way, it wasn't very classy, was it?"

"Whatever, Józef. You can't hurt me anymore. I am sure you realize by now I am the one holding all the cards. If not, you wouldn't have contacted me," I said, trying to sound more confident than I was feeling.

"Ah, Francesca. Don't get too confident. Things are never as they seem. Now tell me where the files on NICO are."

We paused while the woman sitting beside Józef got up, presumably to go to the washroom. I looked back at Józef.

"Why should I tell you? What would I gain from that?" I asked, watching to make sure his female companion was indeed going into the ladies room before I looked back at him.

Józef sat staring at me without blinking. It was as if he was telepathically invading my head. I felt his eyes bore into mine. I blinked and turned my head.

"Listen, Józef. Those files are the only thing keeping me alive right now. I have nothing left. Nothing. It is my only lifeline. If I give them to you, I'm dead."

"All I want is a copy," he offered. "But I want it today."

I felt the panic creeping back in. I knew my face always betrayed me. Would he figure out I truly didn't have the proof? I was hoping this time my face would not deceive me.

"No," I stated. "I have no reason to help you. Why would I ever help you?"

Józef cleared his throat, took a long sip of his coffee and said, "Have you seen your friend Marianne today?"

I swallowed hard.

"What have you done with her, Józef?" I said, in a slow and deliberate tone.

But Józef never replied. He stared directly at me, only now he had a vacant expression on his face. A moment later, I knew why. He slumped over onto the table and exposed the bullet hole in the back of his head. Amongst the incredible din circulating around the food court packed with dozens of patrons, I knew it would have been next to impossible to hear a shot if it was muffled by a silencer.

CHAPTER 60

I leapt to my feet and walked as fast as I could without trying to call any undue attention to myself. I had made it almost 50 feet when I heard the screams. Józef's companion must have returned to the table. I was practically running now. What the hell happened? Who the hell shot Józef? I looked around as I made my way outside just before I bolted to my car. I got in and turned the engine over, barely believing I got back to it without incident. Surely the food court was crawling with security by now. But that wasn't my concern at the moment. All I could think about was Marianne.

At first, I had no idea what to think or where to go. Then I thought the most logical place to start would be her house. I decided to head straight there and see if Józef left behind any clues as to where he had taken her. As I drove back along The Linc, I kept praying she would still be alive, wherever she was.

Marianne lived in Oakville, and her house was only twenty minutes from where I was. I sped along the highway as quickly as I could trying desperately not to get pulled over. A speeding ticket was the last thing I needed.

"Please be okay. Please be okay," I kept repeating, over and over.

I couldn't believe Józef was actually dead. I knew his days were numbered. Too many people wanted him dead. But shot right in front of me? I never saw that one coming. So much for my game plan, I thought. All I wanted to do was get him arrested to stall for time.

As I drove down Marianne's street, I decided to park several houses down and walk to her house. As I quietly approached her driveway, I looked up at her windows. There was no movement, so I walked up the pathway towards her front door and peered through the etched glass. I wanted to open up her garage door to see if her car was still there, but on the off chance she was in the house with some of Józef's men, I didn't want to alert them to my presence.

Should I call the authorities? I wondered. No, I couldn't. What was I thinking? I was probably wanted for questioning right about now. I am sure Józef's female companion would have told the police about me. Then again, Józef may have never told her who I was. He never readily shared information with people, especially females. One way or the other, I couldn't take the chance.

Perhaps I should just ring the bell, make sure no one is inside, and then enter through the backdoor. I knew where Marianne kept her spare key, so entry wouldn't be difficult at all. Then I could begin to look for clues.

I rang the doorbell and waited. Two minutes later, I heard someone descending the staircase. I started to panic, but the door was opened before I could think of what to do next. I couldn't believe my eyes.

It was Marianne.

CHAPTER 61

"Mare!" I yelled, grabbing her and hugging her. "Are you okay?"

"Frankie, what are you doing here?" she asked, looking a bit bewildered.

"Can I come in?"

"Of course," she said, stepping back so I could walk around her.

"My god, I thought Józef had kidnapped you," I said. "You have no idea how relieved I am to see you. You will never believe what I have just been through. You are just never going to believe it."

I was rambling, and I knew it.

"Frankie. Calm down. Tell me what the hell is going on. All of it."

Marianne and I walked up the hardwood stairs and into her sitting room. The walls were filled with autographed photos of famous writers and some of her publishing awards. I sat down on the edge of her overstuffed lavender sofa and began to explain what happened at the mall. She sat there fixated by my every word. Again, I had to avoid telling her about NICO, but thought I did quite a good job avoiding it. Lying seemed to be becoming second nature to me. It was a thought that didn't sit well with me at all. After I finished explaining the whole event to her, I stood up to turn on the news. It was almost six o'clock.

"Hang on, Mare. I want to see if Józef's murder made the news yet."

I sat back down on the sofa and turned up the volume with the remote. After ten minutes, the anchorman had finished up discussing local events and was now moving on to the world stage. I couldn't believe it. Where was the shooting? Why wasn't it being covered? Then it occurred to me. What if it was being covered up? What if the agency stepped in and took charge of the situation. That would certainly explain the lack of news coverage. If it was a mob hit, I would have definitely made the headlines.

"It must have been agency intervention, Mare. That's the only explanation. What do you think?" I asked, turning to look at her.

But the look on her face was bizarre. She looked perplexed and almost scared.

"Marianne? What's wrong?" I asked, standing up to approach her.

"Frankie. What are you not telling me? We have been friends for a long time. I know you are in trouble, yes, but I also know you are not telling me the truth about everything."

I stared at her for a moment.

"Marianne, you are going to have to trust me on this one. Yes, I am not telling you everything, but it's for your own safety. Please. Trust me."

Marianne stood up and walked over to her desk. She stood facing it, her back to me.

"Mare, what's wrong?"

I could feel it. My gut told me something was terribly wrong.

"What the hell is going on, Mare?" I said, starting to back away from her.

"Frankie. The government contacted me," she began, still refusing to face me. "You are in serious trouble. They told me about Thomas too. I know everything. You have to turn yourself in."

"WHAT?" I bellowed. "What the hell did they tell you?"

"I know Thomas was wanted for espionage. I know he had information he was going to give to the other side. I know he has conned you into helping him in his sick web of deceit. They told me everything, Frankie. For your own safety, you have to give yourself up."

"No, Marianne. You have it all wrong."

Marianne turned around before responding to me this time.

"I don't think so, Frankie. I think you are in over your head. I think you fell for the wrong man and now you can't think clearly."

"NO! Trust me on this. They lied to you. Those are the men from the agency I told you about. The one's who killed Thomas."

"Frankie, the men from the government showed up with local officials. They had documents, photographs, video tape. I'm afraid Thomas has been lying to you from the beginning, and now he is still using you to do his bidding even after he is gone. Please talk to them. Let them show you all the evidence. They said if you turn yourself in, they will explain everything."

I was shocked. They had gotten to her. They had brainwashed her into believing them.

"Marianne, stop trying to lob balls of logic at me. You've got it all wrong. They have deceived you. I'm leaving now. I'm just going to have to deal with this on my own."

But as I turned to leave, I heard a noise. I turned around to see Marianne holding on to a stun gun.

"Where the hell did you get that!" I bellowed, shocked by Marianne's bizarre actions.

"Frankie, please," she begged. "Just stay and listen to what they have to say. They taught me how to use this. I don't want to, but I will if I have to. You need to listen, and if this is the only way to keep you here, I will take their advice and use it. I don't want to, but I know it's for your own good. It will probably save your life in the long run."

"Are you insane! They are asking you to use a stun gun on me! How is that rational?" I stammered.

"Because it's the only way to keep you out of danger," she tried to reason, her voice a bit unsteady.

"I'm sorry, Mare," I stated, and then I bolted down the stairs towards the front door.

Marianne wasn't sure what to do at first. She wasn't the confrontational type by nature. But ultimately, she ran after me. By the time I made it down the stairs to the front door, she was practically on my heels. I turned to face her.

"Frankie, please!" she begged. "Don't do this. Let them help. Let me help. I'm really scared something bad is going to happen to you."

"I'm leaving, Marianne. That's all there is to it. Now just let me go please. You are wrong about all of this. Why can't you trust me?"

"No, Frankie. You have it all wrong. Thomas was a liar and a con man. Wait until you see what those officials have to show you. It will shed light on everything. You are in denial, Frankie, because you love him. Why can't you trust *me* on this one? I wouldn't hurt you for the world. You know that."

There was no convincing her, so I turned to leave knowing full well she'd try and stop me. I was prepared for it. As she leapt forward, I spun around and kept rotating right past her grabbing her arm in the process and twisting it backwards. I heard her cry out in pain. I immediately let go. It was a knee-jerk reaction. I didn't want to hurt her.

She quickly turned back towards me and swiped at me with the stun gun again. I grabbed her wrist this time, bending it towards her own arm. This time the gun went off and she quickly buckled at the knees and fell to the floor. It was horrible to watch. I began to cry.

"Marianne. I am so sorry. Please forgive me."

I turned and ran out the front door, down the street and into my car, wiping the tears from my face in the process. She never had a chance, I thought. I knew how to defend myself. Marianne did not. The only thing I could do was take solace in the fact that she wasn't truly hurt, only shaken up and momentarily immobile. In about 15 minutes or so, she'd be right as rain and there would be no residuals effects.

I couldn't believe the agency contacted her. When did they speak to her? Did they get to her while I was with Józef or before? Maybe they went to my house and when I wasn't there, they approached her instead? But why? Did they want to see if she knew anything? Maybe they thought if they could get her on their side then I could be detained without a lot of kafuffle. I gave up trying to figure them out. The agency did things for reasons only they were privy to. I would probably never understand their rationale.

As I drove onto the highway, heading back towards Dundas, I began to curse Józef. It was all just a ploy. The fact he didn't kidnap Marianne was irrelevant. He wanted me to know he knew about her and could hurt her if he wanted to. It was his way of controlling the situation and letting me know who was in charge. Ultimately, it turned out to be an exercise in futility. Józef wouldn't be controlling anything anymore.

As I pulled onto my street, I drove past my driveway and into the common parking area for visitors. It wasn't the least conspicuous place to park, but at least my car wasn't in plain view. I decided to go into my house through the back door and quickly grab my emergency passport and carry-on bag. I hadn't bothered to unpack yet, so it still had everything I needed in it to get by.

I wasn't sure where I was going to go; all I knew is I couldn't stay in Ontario. I decided I would drive back out to the airport and figure it all out on my way there.

The *e*-Entity

En route to the Hamilton International Airport, I began to devise a plan. I knew there was always the possibility I was being watched. I just hoped I wasn't right now. It was hard to tell how far I would get, but I had no choice. I could either go back home and wait for the agency to bring me in or flee and hope for the best. I decided if I could get back to the UK, then I could get into Europe quite easily and travel across borders by rented car. I was going to have to stop somewhere along the way and withdraw as much cash as I could from an ATM.

I left my car at a strip mall about two miles out from the airport. I walked into the mall, out through a different exit door, and hailed a cab just in case I was being followed. If I was, I hoped it would buy me some time. I figured any cautionary efforts on my part would be worth it.

Once I was at the airport, I headed towards the ticket booth. It was too bad I had to use the passport the consulate got for me. The officials in Mexico took the fake one Thomas had given me in Sweden. I knew this would make it much easier for the agency to track me to the UK, but I had no choice. All I hoped for now was actually being able to make it onto the plane. The agency still didn't know if I had proof of NICO, and I truly believed this was the only reason I was still alive. If they were here at the airport watching, I didn't think they would risk the possible exposure. As for finding a safe place to hide, I was going to have to get in and out of the UK as quickly as possible.

After I had my ticket in hand, I headed straight for departures. I stood in line for security to examine everyone's bags. The line moved quickly, and I stepped forward and placed my purse and carry-on bag on the conveyor belt to be x-rayed. After stepping through the metal detection archway, I turned to watch the monitor as my belongings went through the machine. After my purse emerged, I watched as my carry-on slid through. I did a double take as a USB Mass Storage device, or flash drive, was illuminated on the screen in the lining of my bag. I tried to stay calm. I tried to keep a relaxed smile on my face for fear of looking guilty of something, but the feeling in the pit of my stomach told me exactly what it was.

CHAPTER 62

The security guard allowed my carry-on bag to go through without incident. I picked up both bags, smiled cordially at the other guards and walked directly to the lounge area. I knew exactly what I was looking for – an Internet kiosk.

My heart was pounding in my throat. I couldn't believe what was happening. How did that storage device get into my bag? I knew there was only one person who had access to it. It was Thomas. He must have put it there sometime during our last trip. I couldn't figure out why he hadn't told me about it, but I was sure he had good reason. I just couldn't believe it had been there the whole time. How could I have missed it? Then it hit me. When I left Mexico, I was escorted and led onto the plane by the consulate representative and the policeman. My bags were checked through by the authorities. They never would have thought anything about the flash drive. It was a common device for people to carry these days. And, I never had time to unpack after I got home. I couldn't believe it had been there all this time.

I found an empty kiosk and used my credit card to obtain credits for the machine. I inserted the flash drive into the port at the side of the computer, double clicked on the G: icon, and found three folders. They were labeled, *e-mails*, *verification*, and *coding*. I opened up the one that read *verification* and watched as thousands of little encryptions filled the screen. It was a beautiful sight. I knew the x-ray machine wouldn't have affected the data. They used carbon nanotube emitters these days which used a lot less energy than conventional x-ray machines.

Smiling, and as quickly as possible, I logged on to my e-mail account. My hands were shaking as I typed in my password. I opened up a new e-mail window, attached the three files to it, and sent it to myself with a note that read, "Now you know. So leave me the hell alone and nothing will ever go public."

I knew my e-mail was being monitored. I knew the agency would find it. The message was purely for them.

All of a sudden, I felt like the weight of the world had been lifted from me. Now all I had to do was copy the files, hide them in strategic locations and wait for the agency to contact me. They couldn't touch me now, not while I was holding all the cards.

"I love you, Thomas," I said aloud. "I knew you'd come through for me."

I walked back through security and straight out of the airport. I hailed a taxi and took it back to my car. I drove directly to a copy centre, transferred all the data onto two CDs, drove across the street to the post office, rented a post office box, dropped one CD through its slot and mailed the other CD to myself at the newspaper I freelanced for. Then I headed home.

As I drove towards Dundas, a profusion of emotions flooded my heart. Yes, I felt a bit relieved, now I actually had proof of NICO in my possession. I felt like I finally had some leverage to negotiate with. I wasn't a fool. I knew the agency wanted me dead. I also knew they would never rest until they found a way to retrieve the evidence I had and eliminate me. I was the last one left.

I glanced at the houses as I drove down my street. They seemed to be gliding past me in slow motion. It was very surreal. I even noticed the sound of a cardinal singing somewhere in the distance. It seemed like forever since my mind was still enough to fathom what else was going on around me. Through all the chaos, through all the heartache, through all the perpetual fear, I was finally beginning to focus again. At last, I was able to breathe. But I wasn't stupid. I knew I wouldn't be safe for long. I knew I had only bought myself a small amount of time.

That theory was totally qualified when I drove up to my house and noticed a strange Buick with tinted windows parked a few doors down. I wasn't worried. I knew it was only an intimidation tactic. I was getting used to it.

I parked in my driveway, got out of my car, turned towards the Buick, smiled and waved as I walked up to my front door. I would have flipped them off but my grandmother told me it wasn't very ladylike the last time she saw me do it.

I climbed the stairs and headed straight for the kitchen and poured myself a large glass of my Wolf Blass. I took a huge gulp, looked down at my glass, and started to sob. I have no idea how long I stood there. It was like every ounce of hurt and anger came pouring out of me all at once. I think my mind finally realized I was at last in a position to grieve. I never tried to hold back any of the tears, but I think they would have come out nonetheless. Physically or mentally the human body could endure a lot, but it always had to be followed by some sort of release. It was part of the healing process.

I had lost so many people in my life and now Thomas was gone as well. I had always wondered if I would be capable of having a great love. Sometimes, because of what I had endured in my past, I truly didn't believe I deserved it. Other times I felt like I did but never really allowed myself to venture there for fear of getting hurt. Either way, it didn't matter because now I knew. When it's the right person, anything is possible.

I thought about Marianne as well. I knew we would get past this, but I also knew it would be some time before those fences could be mended. I wasn't about to drop her right back in this. It was better if I kept my distance for the time being.

When the tears finally subsided, I walked into my living room and sat down on the couch with a second glass of wine in my hand. I thought about the agency and their diligent minions who were, in all probability, frantically running around trying to figure out a way to take me down. There was one thing, though, that was abundantly clear to me. I had to figure out a way to get myself out of this whole situation before they got to me.

ONE WEEK LATER

It was a beautiful autumn day, and I had just returned from an exhilarating 4km run up and down the escarpment. I stopped to catch my breath and retrieve my mail out of my postbox.

"Nothing but bills," I said aloud.

I looked around. No Buick today. I unlocked my front door and took the stairs two by two all the way up to the top floor and into my bedroom. I was in dire need of a hot shower. Just as I started to pull some clean clothes out of my armoire to change into, I heard the chime of my doorbell and made my way to the front door and opened it.

"Alejandro, please come in."

"It is always a pleasure, Frankie," he said, kissing me on both cheeks and stepping into the foyer.

I motioned for him to follow me upstairs. "Can I make you a tea or coffee? Something a bit stronger, perhaps?"

"I am fine, thank you," he said, sitting down on the chair next to the sliding glass doors.

I sat down on the couch across from him.

"You said you wanted to talk to me about something?"

"I do," I said. "I'll get straight to the point. I want to go after the agency."

Alejandro stared at me for a moment.

"Are you sure about this?" he asked.

"Yes, I am. If I don't make the first move, it is only a matter of time before they come after me."

Alejandro eyed me very carefully.

"Before you ask, yes, I have the proof. Will you help me?" I asked.

I knew Alejandro would be able to help me. I never did find out what his connection to Thomas was. All I knew was he was well connected, knew the same people Thomas did, and was the only one left I could trust, comparatively of course. Nonetheless, I wasn't about to emphatically trust anyone.

"I have a way of getting you into the agency, if that is truly what you wish to do."

I never asked how. I didn't think I really wanted to know.

"I had a feeling you would, and yes, it is truly what I wish to do," I said.

"Thomas was like a brother to me."

"I know."

He stood up and walked over to me.

"If this is the path you are choosing, then there is something else you need to see."

He handed me a folded piece of newspaper.

"What is this?" I asked, as I began to unfold it.

"Please, just open it."

I did as he requested. It was a newspaper article from Mexico.

"I am sorry, but I don't understand what it says."

"It is from exactly nine days ago. It says there was an unidentified burn victim admitted to a hospital just outside of Cancun."

I looked up at Alejandro, not saying a word.

"I went to the hospital, but he was no longer there," he said.

"Alejandro, there is no way," I said, very slowly.

"There are a lot of coincidences to the story, Frankie."

"It is not possible. I saw the explosion. I was there. No one could have survived that kind of blast."

Alejandro looked down at me as a grin began to spread across his face.

"Whoso loves, believes the impossible."